A
HAUNTED
SYMPHONY

A NOVEL

A

HAUNTED

SYMPHONY

A NOVEL

Written by:

Michele Wallace Campanelli

International Best-selling Author

ARPress
45 Dan Road Suite 5
Canton MA 02021

Hotline: 1(888) 821-0229
Fax: 1(508) 545-7580

Ordering Information:

Quantity sales. Special discounts are available on quantity purchases by corporations, associations, and others. For details, contact the publisher at the address above.

Printed in the United States of America.

ISBN-13:   Paperback   979-8-89330-449-7
                eBook   979-8-89330-450-3
                Hardback   979-8-89330-451-0

Library of Congress Control Number: 2024901763

TABLE OF CONTENTS

*Praise him with the **strings** and pipe.* **-Psalm 150:4**

This book is dedicated to all those who love music.

I want to thank my late husband, Louie, and especially my mother, Fontaine, who is my friend and an editor. Also, I appreciate the moral support from my brother David, Greg, Melisa & Dick, Dawn & Ben Kreiselman, Sherry MacLean, the entire Wallace & Campanelli family, and especially Director Aaron Collins with the Space Coast Symphony Orchestra and Director Robert Lamb with the Brevard Community College Chorale and BSO. Concerts and performances with these orchestras have inspired much of the symphony music mentioned in this novel.

To God be the glory!

CHAPTER 1

Don't go in there!

I heard the music librarian shriek as my hand touched the doorknob; her voice stopped me from turning the handle. I turned to face her, and the look she gave warned of dire consequences.

She was an attractive woman in her sixties; her gray hair bobbed to her shoulders, and she wore a Florida sundress. It was her eyes that had sunken in that made me realize how serious she was, along with her pursed lips and raised brows.

"The sun has gone down," she said. "We don't let volunteers in the library after dark."

"What's in there?" I asked, confused. I remember that this was my third visit to the symphony office as a volunteer, and I'd never seen anyone but her enter. "Treasure?"

She straightened the skirt of her colorful sundress as she left her desk and walked over to me. "The music in there is worth thousands upon thousands of dollars. The conductor and I are the only ones allowed in."

"She's lying," came from another volunteer folding the programs for tomorrow night's concert. "That's not the reason. Tell her! Tell her! She won't believe you anyway."

"No need --if she never goes in the library."

I realized I had forgotten her name. "I'm sorry…"

"My name's Jenny, Jennifer Miller." She stopped folding and looked straight at me. "I am the Music Librarian for the

Symphony. I must ensure the music gets shipped out to our musicians in time for them to learn it before each concert. That's sometimes up to 60 musicians."

"That has nothing to do with what's in the library," the other volunteer stopped folding her programs, too. "My name is Karen Jacobs; I am on the Board. We have a problem in the library of the supernatural kind. We hardly ever discuss it. Two years ago, when I first came to the symphony, I made the mistake of going there at night. I needed a solo piece for a vocalist who had phoned saying she never got her copy of the music. I went in and…"

"Stop it!" Jennifer warned. "No need to scare a new volunteer. She might not come back."

I took a deep breath and realized whatever was behind that door must be frightening. "I don't scare easy now. A few years back, I lost my husband of ten years to cancer."

"The concertmaster violinist in Georgia," Jennifer knew. "We tried to get him as a special guest but couldn't book him."

"Yes," my eyes showed the pain. "He was very hard to book, always so busy performing worldwide, and then he had his students as well. He loved all of them, so I finally decided to move down to Florida, to the Space Coast. I would run into his students all over town, and they loved him so much that some would burst into tears when they saw me. I needed a fresh start. At least, that's what my counselor suggested. I sold my house and moved into an apartment locally," I added.

"But you came here to volunteer?" Karen said, surprised. "What is your name?"

"I missed the music and being around musicians," I admitted. "My name is Maria Wilson. I have also done a lot of marketing, especially social media. I did that professionally and have a communication degree."

"My goodness, do we need help with social media!" Karen gasped. "I will tell Charles to put you on our marketing team."

"I was on the Georgia Symphony board and worked behind the scenes with promotion and social media. I can't ever get my husband back, but I can be around the music and do what I love. Marketing concerts always gave me so much joy, as did playing the violin. Sometimes, I sang in the choir, too. That's how I met him. I had this grand notion of someday playing a violin. He was my teacher, and after our first lesson, I knew he was the man I wanted to marry. The way he looked at me," my voice softened.

"Well, it's an honor to have you here," Jenny said. "You'll do just fine here."

"Our conductor is quite handsome and single," Karen giggled.

"That he is," voiced another volunteer across the room.

"He was engaged last year to some actress, but she dumped him. Can you imagine? Dumped him for some star in Hollywood. He was devastated and hasn't dated anyone since. You should meet him!" Karen grabbed the program and showed me the Conductor's photo. He was holding a baton, and his smile lit up the page. His facial features were rugged, and his eyes sparked bright blue. His yellow-streaked blonde hair brought out the color of his gems. Wearing a tuxedo, he was undoubtedly as handsome as they claimed.

"Wow!" escaped my lips.

"Wow, is right!" Jennifer laughed. "Half of our volunteers have a crush on him. We never have a problem with getting volunteers, either. Have you ever seen our Conductor in person? He looks hotter than Chris Pine, Tom Hiddleston, Jason Momoa, Henry Cavill, or Chris Hemsworth."

"Superhero hot?" I blushed, my smile brightening.

"Super talented as well," Karen mumbled.

Remembering how we started talking, I repeated, "So what's in the music library?"

"Just lots of filing cabinets and a chair," Jennifer nodded, wiping the sweat from her forehead, "I am the only one allowed in because of the worth of music. Most people don't know that one piece of music for sixty musicians can cost over a grand."

"Oh, I do," I brightened. "My late husband spent a fortune on music. He loved rare pieces."

"What did you do with it?" Jenny asked.

"Donated it all to the Georgia Symphony in his honor," I admitted, shrugging, "I play violin a little but nowhere near good enough to play what he could. I sing now, mostly."

"You should audition for us," Karen leaned forward.

"Not sure I am that good," my cheeks reddened with a quizzical look, "But I have a feeling it isn't just music in there. What is paranormal?"

"We are not sure how it happened. It may have come when we acquired some music. Some of our pieces of music are vintage and have been around a hundred years or so, but somehow, something came with them. We don't know exactly how or why. We are just guessing that's the cause. We've also had many musicians die over the years, one or two by suicide or drug overdose," her voice dropped.

"That's awful," I gasped at the news.

"We have a ghost," Jennifer finally revealed.

"A ghost," slight disbelieving giggles rose in my throat.

"Not a friendly one either," Karen said, barely able to nod. "Whoever it is likes to scare anyone who enters that room at night."

"I only go inside during the day," Jennifer admitted, peering directly into my eyes. "Even then, I feel it watching me."

"Really?" I still didn't believe it. "I'm sorry. I don't believe in ghosts. If there were such a thing, my husband George would have visited me at least once since he died of cancer. That was never the case."

Karen approached and wrapped her arm around me with her other hand, scooping the necklace away from her neck. "It doesn't matter if you believe in ghosts because whatever is there will believe in you. Best you don't go in there."

"Ever!" Jennifer warned, then hesitated to say, "Trust me. Never go in there at night."

I smiled and walked back to the table to help fold programs. "All right, whatever you ladies say; I'm just a volunteer these days and want free admission to watch the concerts. Widows must watch their budgets."

Jenny and Karen stepped closer to the table.

"Thank you for being a volunteer. We wouldn't survive without them." Karen added.

"I know," I sighed. "It's hard for any symphony to manage these days. My husband was as famous as Joshua Bell, and we just managed every year thanks to his students."

"We should have ghost tours," Karen suggested. "We'd make more money selling tickets to a ghost tour."

I lowered my eyes, knowing that she was probably right. Music can be a challenging profession, even for the very talented.

CHAPTER 2

It was not a good hair day. Maria brushed her hair quickly, checking once if her raven mane was parted correctly before sitting in her office chair. A red-haired, blue-eyed man walked into her home office apartment. He was strikingly handsome with his extensive Irish-looking features. With a glance down to see if he was wearing a wedding ring she suddenly put down her hairbrush, "Good morning, Ms. Wilson."

"Good morning, you are Charles McDaniel with the symphony?"

"Yes, call me Charlie. I am so pleased you could fit me into your busy schedule this morning, Ms. Wilson. Karen recommended you for our social media position. She said that if the symphony still needed a Social Media Director, you would be the very person capable. I certainly can maintain Twitter, Facebook, Instagram, and possible Pinterest accounts for the symphony."

"Yes, you were a Georgia Symphony Orchestra Board Member?" Charlie asked, his voice lowering between his teeth. "I'm surprised you don't already have a Social Media Director set up for such a large orchestra."

"We do have a website, but our Director, Henry Coggins, who is also the founder of the orchestra, has used mostly newspaper advertising. Our marketing needs to be more progressive to reach a younger audience." Charles McDaniel sat down in the chair opposite Marie's black leather sofa. "Jana Mires has gotten Board approval to hire you if you are interested in the position. I was told you are a singer and a musician as well."

"I do sing some in choirs," Maria blushed, plastering a smile. "Sometimes for churches and I play a little violin."

"Good, then you understand the importance of music." Charles grabbed the tip of his red goatee and then raised a hand. "Have you ever been to one of our symphony concerts?"

"No, I'm afraid not."

"The PSO is the largest music organization on the coast. We employ over a hundred musicians and singers. We do more than 22 concerts per year. All that must be marketed online."

"Do you have a graphic artist on staff?" Maria questioned, staring at him.

"Yes," he chuckled, nodding. "Although she is a bit out there. I think she's a space alien; her hair is all different colors."

Maria glanced at him and laughed, "I see you have a sense of humor, Mr. McDaniels."

"Heather is quite good, though. Works from home and emails in the graphics. We send her art into the newspapers so she understands sizing and pixels."

"Excellent," Maria smiled. "She will be a great resource to begin online marketing and help me build a social media fan-base for the Palms Symphony Orchestra."

"Are you single?" he asked, holding his breath until she answered. "I must ask."

I blushed, then smiled. "Well, yes."

"Our Artistic Director -Conductor Henry Coggins," Charles said, wrinkling his nose. "All the ladies seem to find him attractive. I don't want any distractions."

"I assure you, your Conductor is just a client to me. I am quite professional."

"Good. We don't need you to be distracted." Charles said. "Also, Jennifer, our PSO Librarian has a big imagination. So don't let her ghost stories scare you. She wants no one to go into the library because sheet music is precious. Karen also told me she's already tried to scare you with made-up ghost tales."

"She did, but that's okay. I don't believe in ghosts anyway." I chuckled softly as I remembered.

"When can you start?" Charles asked. He swiveled in his seat to glare at me. "I was very impressed after talking to the Georgia Symphony."

"Today. I will search your website and look for upcoming concerts and set up a meeting with Jana Mires. PR and social media often work together to get the best possible marketing campaign set up, one that coincides. Does the PSO have regular marketing meetings?"

"Jana will tell you all about them if you intend to come. I am very pleased that you will be on board," Charles added, standing back up.

"It will be my pleasure," I stood and shook his hand.

"Wilson. Your last name is Wilson, isn't it?" Charles McDaniel questioned. "Are you any relation to that renowned lawyer Donnie Wilson?"

I squinted, not wanting to admit it. My chest suddenly tightened. "Yes, he is my brother, but we hardly ever see each other."

"What a shame," Charles McDaniel shook his head. "I was very impressed with his representing that model who went on a shooting spree. Oh…not Kardashian, who was that model?"

"Amanda Stones," I said. "And he was able to get her off even though she was drunk while driving and shot a man."

Charles McDaniel took a step back. "He might want to talk to Jana about setting up some advertisements for his law firm. Our programs host many advertisers of that caliber."

"Next time I see him, I'll mention it," Maria said, her gaze lingering. "Thank you so much for coming in."

"Well, talk again very soon," Charles tagged; then he left, shutting the door to her studio-home office.

CHAPTER 3

Jana Mires was ordering a cup of Joe at the coffee shop when I entered the café. I recognized her immediately because her business and face appeared in every playbill, program, and newspaper across this city.

Dressed to the nines, Jana had blonde hair, perfect makeup, and a gold purse matching her golden stilettoes. She handed the sales clerk a ten-dollar bill and murmured, "Keep the change." On a heel, she pivoted and loaded her coffee with cream on the counter, then glanced in my direction.

Jana's eyes widened, and in a smile with perfectly white teeth, said, "Oh, my, I just got an email about you from Charlie. He said you would be the perfect candidate for our social media position."

I steadied myself and raised a hand for Jana to shake.

Jana Mires immediately set her coffee on a small two-seater table and returned the gesture. "Would you care to join me? I have a few questions for you, if you don't mind, Ms. Wilson, right? Not Mrs.? You are the sister of that big-time Hollywood lawyer."

"I am his sister," I sat down. "I'll join you if you have some inquiries. Call me, Maria."

"Can I get you a cup?" Jana asked, pointing to her mug.

"I am here to pick up a book," I replied, pointing to a bookshelf with paperbacks for sale underneath a sign that read for "2 for $20." "But I do have some time before my next appointment."

"Great," Jana said.

I took a moment to look over Jana as she fumbled through her purse and pulled out a pen. Jana Mires was significantly put together. It was obvious that she had money, and she knew how to show it. Even the sunglasses on her face had diamonds crusted on the sides and the case she quickly threw in looked designer.

"You are single, right?" Jana asked, stirring her coffee until the cream mixed.

"Yes," I nodded.

"Okay, how can I put this…I only have one problem with hiring you. And it really isn't a problem because the Georgia Symphony recommends you. Also, I know Jason Shannon and he highly praises you. Your social media networking saved his tire company. That idea of a free oil change was brilliant."

"Just have to purchase two tires," I blurted out.

"Excellent, I love that type of thinking." Jana's blue eyes flickered. "I've seen your photography as well. You certainly have an eye; not everyone can make a tire look interesting."

"So, what is the problem?" I wondered with the cold air from an air conditioning vent prickling my neck and shoulder.

"Well, our conductor, Henry is also single," Jana said, her blue eyes tightening.

"Charles McDaniels also hinted along these lines, and I assure you that I am the most professional woman you will ever know."

"Henry is very attractive," Jana said, her cheeks reddening. "He's tall. He's smart and most women find him interesting as well. He founded this orchestra and in the past few years he's taken it all the way to performing in the largest auditoriums the Space Coast has. He's quite the catch and named one of the top four bachelors in our state."

"I am not going to step out of line," I said, strongly.

"That's what they all say, Dear," Jana forced a smile. "Of course you are a little different than most. You are successful and attractive yourself."

"What exactly are you worried about?" I shrugged my shoulders.

"Well don't say that I didn't warn you," Jana sipped more of her coffee. "Now our first meeting is next week, and it will be quite intensive. Henry has just announced next season so we need to discuss a marketing plan for season tickets and structure a schedule for the first concert which I believe is in June."

"June?" I raised my brows. "So PSO is year-round?"

"Yes, we aren't the typical symphony, and a huge part of our revenue comes during the summer when other orchestras are usually on summer break. Henry has really made this orchestra very successful by not competing with other concerts, so as you can see this is quite a job you are taking on. You are expected to build us a fan base that will purchase tickets year-round. Although, with your track record of turning around companies, I can see you are quite capable."

"You only doubt that I will remain professional?" I forced a grin.

"Oh, Henry is very personable. Charlie has been his friend since college. We are very much like a family. You will see that formalities are often forgotten about, and Henry is very likable. There will be many who see you with him and immediately wonder if you might be dating him."

"I will immediately correct them," I responded quickly.

"Yes, but not all women are pleasant when they have a crush on Henry. You are attractive enough that they won't want you around him," Jana announced, then stood and trotted out with her cup of Joe. "I warned you. See you next week," she added as she exited.

CHAPTER 4

I pressed the speed dial button on my Betty Boop cell phone and waited as the phone on the other end kept ringing. "Hello, you have reached the office of Don Wilson. I'm out of the office; please leave a message."

Beep.

"Hi, Donnie, it's your sister. I just wanted to update you on all that's going on with Mom and me. I haven't heard from you for quite some time. I know you are busy but please return my call when you can. Bye."

I stuffed the cell phone inside my purse and walked into a building labeled C Government. As I strolled by, reading the numbers on the doors, I saw an open door and two ladies standing at the entrance.

"Good morning," said the tall blonde. "Are you here for the Social Media workshop put on by the Business Alliance?"

"Yes," I answered with my smile fading.

"Welcome. Here is your packet. May I take your name and sign you in," the stranger exclaimed.

"I am Maria Wilson."

"Oh, yes! We've got a seat for you right next to Jana Mires," she said, her dark eyes lighting up.

"Really?" I scanned the room and saw Jana sitting at the end of a long, narrow table. She was tapping her phone with her right hand and drinking a cup of coffee with her left. A seat was open beside her. "Thank you."

I strolled in front of the tables and sat down next to Jana. It was hard not to notice the smell of designer perfume and that the dress she was wearing looked like it had come right off a New York runway; it was a light blue and A-line. This woman had an incredible figure with petite-perfect features, and thick, short blonde hair. Jana could be a model, she was so strikingly beautiful, eloquent, and refined.

"I saved you a seat," Jana said, her voice strong but very feminine. "Charlie told me he sent you this morning. Congratulations on your official new position as social media Director of the PSO!"

"Yes, thank you," I responded, my mouth slightly open.

"This will fill up fast, and I figured you'd want to be closer to the front." Jana smiled with white teeth that glistened as she spoke. "Terry is great. You'll love this seminar."

"You've been here before?"

"Goes on about three times a year. My PR company is one of the sponsors for the event and we like to invite those who are up and coming, the real movers and shakers in the community." Jana explained. "It helps us Media folks to stay in contact and network."

"I see," I nodded, realizing how important this event was for networking.

"You know about the marketing meeting later this week with the PSO? I sent you a text."

"I will be there."

Jana put down her cup slowly and gracefully. "You need to meet the rest of the marketing staff and begin as soon as possible. The PSO has two concerts next month, and one includes a chorus. We'll need you to spread the word to the local singers composing a chorus."

"Do you have a list of singers?"

"We don't. The Choral Director was fired and felt that the list of email addresses was his to keep. I've tried to get a hold of him, and he isn't releasing them. So, we may need to get the word out and to alert our singers to show up for rehearsal."

"Won't that be insulting to them not to be contacted directly?" I asked, choking out the question. "It will appear as if they weren't invited."

"Yes, that is a possibility," Jana said, sipping more coffee.

"The Choral Director for the PSO was Brian Allen, correct?"

"His day job is as a Choir Director for that Community Church on 5th Ave." Jana briefly touched my arm. "You'd think a Music Minister wouldn't steal the PSO list of professional singers, but that is what happened. He claims the names he gathered and put together were for his church, not the PSO."

I smirked, raising a brow. "Did he now? Did Charles mention to you that I am a singer?"

"Yes, and a little violin, too," Jana said. "I'm a second soprano, and luckily, I know many of the singers on his list. I will ensure they are invited, but we have lost many names and email addresses. Henry didn't keep a master list because he trusted that Brian Allen would remain as our director. He never questioned his behavior until he quit directing the New Time Jazz Band Singers. His real love is jazz music, and he found it a better opportunity."

Suddenly, an Asian woman with long brownish-black hair entered the room and stood before the tables. I glanced back and found that there wasn't even one seat open; most people there were women. Two older gentlemen sat in the back. Everyone in the room had a laptop computer except Jana.

I realized that Jana should have brought a laptop computer instead of her paper notebook. At least Jana and I thought alike, not needing a computer, and she wasn't the only one without one.

"Good morning," greeted the Asian woman. "My name is Terry Newman, and I am from Communication Inkwell. I will be your host for this Social Media Workshop. Today, we will discuss the differences in the Social Media platforms and their demographics."

From the back, a gentleman wearing a three-piece suit raised his hand. "Ms. Newman, how long will this workshop be?"

"Typically, my workshops run a little over two hours with a question-and-answer section at the end for those who want to stay."

"I may have to leave early," he said disappointedly.

"Feel free to leave whenever you need to," Terry Newman continued. "Now we all know that Facebook and Twitter lead the pack with users. The next three may surprise you.

We have LinkedIn, Pinterest, and Instagram. Let's begin with PowerPoint on Pinterest. The demographic for Pinterest is 30–60-year-old women, particularly mothers."

My eyes tightened in surprise.

Jana leaned over, "The PSO isn't that interested in Pinterest because of that."

"What about the children's programs?" I questioned.

"We do put those on a few times a year. Henry loves animated film scores, so we might be able to use Pinterest for those," Jana sighed, "although, there was a big disappointment in the turnout last year. I don't think we hit the designated target audience since most of our emailed newsletters are going out to our season ticket holders who are older."

"I see," I nodded.

Terry Newman's eyes focused on Jana. "We'll talk afterward. I better shut up and while Terry gives her workshop," Jana smiled at Maria. With that, Jana leaned back in her chair and didn't say another word during the rest of the Social Media Workshop.

I listened to Terry Newman. Now and again she would jot down a note and smile at Jana, who continued to sip her coffee.

After several hours of listening, the workshop ended with loud applause for Terry Newman. "Now if any of you have questions, please stay afterward and I will be free to answer. Please don't be shy; this is your opportunity to ask me something."

"Are you going to stay?" I asked Jana.

"There is nothing she can teach me. I already know enough about marketing to write a book," Jana said. "But you stay. I'll see you at the PSO marketing meeting later this week." Then Jana rose and walked out the door with her blue stilettos clicking against the tiled floor. With a gentle turn of her slender wrist, she tossed her empty coffee cup into the trash.

CHAPTER 5

I approached the simple two-story complex beside a river. The water was calm today, with no breeze disturbing the silver oak branches. Quickly, I passed the sign out front of the building, Palm Symphony Orchestra, over smaller black letters, Conductor Henry Collins—second Floor.

I walked to the front of what was once initially a historic two-story brick Florida home. It had a small porch and glass doors; it was quite a beautiful building. After climbing three stairs, I noticed the bronze statue of a monkey holding a violin with a grin. *Interesting.* I wondered how I missed the monkey in the garden area the last time I'd come to volunteer. I hit the doorbell with a quick jab and waited until the door opened halfway.

"Yes," said a woman in her early thirties.

I recognized her as one of the cello soloists with a short, bobbed haircut and beautiful green eyes that I'd seen in the newspaper. "Kerry Bartwell?"

"Yes, and you must be our new marketing team member, Maria," Kerry added. "Go past Jennifer's desk and the library, right up those stairs, and the boardroom to the left. The meeting will start in a few minutes. Henry is running late."

Moving on, I smelled solid lavender perfume. I walked past Jenny's desk, and the door marked library. The second I moved past the library, a chill went up my spine, remembering that Jennifer had warned me about a ghost. I quickly dismissed the eerie feeling as my finger immediately went to my nose to avoid a sneeze. I hurried and sneezed up the stairs when I got to the top.

"God bless you," Kerry said with a quick nod.

It was then I realized Kerry had followed me. "Thank you."

"I am also on the marketing team but mostly I work on parties. I am a certified party planner."

"That is part of the marketing team?" I asked, raising a brow.

"Honey, that got me to the Board. Party planning is a huge part of marketing the orchestra." Kerry informed, clutching a notebook. "Now, follow me. I'll show you where to go. It's just around the corner."

Kerry led me down a long hallway, past a door-marked bathroom, and then into a room the size of the average bedroom. In the center was a long wooden table surrounded by ten chairs. Only three were filled: Jana Mires sat at the head, and two other ladies sat opposite her.

"Hi, I'm Lisa Appleseed. You must be Maria Wilson," said the blonde directly opposite of Jana. "I'm the Palms Symphony Orchestra's secretary. Welcome."

"It is an honor to be your Social Media Director," I stated passionately.

Kerry sat down next to Jana, and I followed her to sit beside her.

"Long time no see," Jana said as she opened a notepad. "That was some workshop."

Pondering, "I enjoyed learning more about Instagram.

That is the platform I'm ready to dive into."

"For the young 35-year-olds or teenagers," Jana said, taking a pen off the table. "Not really our demographic, but we have a link to our Instagram account on our website. Henry will give you all the passwords and social media account usernames so you can begin uploading advertisements and photos."

"Do you take photographs?" asked Kerry, studying Maria's face.

I admitted. "I use mostly a professional Cannon DOS 5D Mark IV camera; for low light, I have a Nikon and then a GoPro to get action videos."

"Wouldn't GoPro look unprofessional?" asked Kerry, her eyes widening.

"Tests have proven that unprofessional videos are the highest clicked on Facebook. Professional videos tend to be seen as advertisements, so people scroll past them," Jana added. "Last season, the PSO spent $7,000 on a short video advertisement, and it only got 200 likes even after boosting it! The GoPro video Henry's cousin took for free of the trombone section from the floor got over 3,000 likes and over 24,000 views, and it didn't cost a thing," Jana huffed. "I'm glad we'll have a GoPro on the team."

"Do you think Henry would wear a helmet and the GoPro while conducting? Now that would be cool!" Kerry smiled, sitting up in her chair.

"I could set that up," I nodded.

Suddenly, loud footsteps came up the stairs. A shadow

crossed the back of the wall.

Jana opened her notebook. "Let's hope the meeting doesn't last three hours this time."

"It might. I must discuss the season opener party. I'm not even sure what he wants on the menu or on the tables. He discussed symphony photos as centerpieces, but I prefer flowers," Kerry said.

In strode a man six feet tall wearing jeans and a button-down shirt. A baseball cap with the Nike swoosh was on his head. He removed his oversized sunglasses, and I saw Henry Collins in person for the first time.

He glanced around the room and then stopped at me.

"Hello," I caught my breath.

Henry grabbed the chair at the head of the table and slowly sat down. He plopped a briefcase next to his chair but stared at me.

"I am Maria Wilson. Charlie McDaniels…"

"I know who you are," Henry said firmly. "I just hadn't prepared myself for how beautiful you are."

How embarrassing! I was speechless as the women in the room stared as much as Henry did.

"Married?" Henry asked with a grin.

"No," I whispered.

"Maybe I have a chance then," he said, widening his grin.

My heart started pounding. My gaze moved to my

notebook, and I opened and grabbed a pen resting beside it. When I finally composed myself, I glanced over, and yes, Henry was still staring at me.

"Such a flirt," Jana rolled her eyes.

That handsome man is worth marrying.

CHAPTER 6

"I am sorry to say that I have another meeting in about thirty minutes so that I will make this brief. Ms. Wilson, I want to build a bigger symphony fan base on Twitter, Facebook, and I, Instagram. Start that immediately with graphic ads of our upcoming concert. You take photos as well, right?"

"Yes," Maria smiled, shaking her head.

"Great, come to rehearsals and concerts and take photos from the sides, backstage, wherever necessary."

"I'll do my best not to disturb the audience and performers," Maria said, her smile fading.

"Your camera doesn't make noise, does it?" he asked, raising his brows.

"I can shut the clicking off."

"Good and no flash photography," he kept staring at her.

"My Nikon camera does well in low light and I have a zoom, so it shouldn't be a problem for me."

He straightened in his chair and brushed his blonde streaked hair with a hand, then tapped his pencil. "I hate to be in photographs. Honestly, I'm not one for photo shoots, but I realize this is necessary to promote the concerts and sell tickets. I'm trying to reach out to a younger audience and if the board passes my request, I'll promote the free concerts mostly online instead of paying for newspaper ads."

"I can understand not wanting to pay for advertisements of free concerts," Maria agreed, sitting back in her chair.

"That's if the board passes your idea," Jana reminded, tapping her pen. "Many on the board feel that we shouldn't do any free concerts because they think it will hurt ticket sales for the surrounding concert dates."

"You know how I feel about that," Henry Coggins finally glared at Jana. "You know what I am after."

"Yes, and your ideas are wonderful, but they won't save the symphony," Jana snapped then jotted a note onto her notepad. "We should be raising prices, not giving away seats."

"I don't have time to argue with you, Jana," he said as he leaned forward. "So, contact the Palmway newspaper, and I'll approve the check."

"Will do," Jana sighed.

"So we will have to set up another meeting, just you and me, Maria."

Maria nodded, hardly able to take her eyes off such a large, handsome, and rugged man.

"The marketing team meets once a month and I'd like a Social Media report on your progress. A page or two should be sufficient. After I see what you can do, we'll meet and discuss any changes that need to be made." Then he turned toward Jana, "I want you to procure the biggest advertisements in the Space Coast Music magazine, both in the classical section and also in the 'Things to Do' list."

"That will be costly," Jana reminded as she set down her pen.

"For both the mag and me," a woman sporting three different hair colors, giant white framed glasses, and a long black dress walked in. She had several tattoos down her arms wrapped halfway up her neck.

"Morning," she saw Maria, and her eyes widened. "I'm Heather, the Graphic Artist for PSO. Welcome to the Marketing team. You're quite beautiful."

"Hello," Maria greeted. "Maria Wilson, Social Media." Remembering what Charles McDaniels' warned, it was all she could do not to whisper, "Heather the alien," under her breath.

"Heather is extremely talented in many areas," Henry announced, winking at Heather.

"And cheap," Heidi added, plopping down in the chair next to Maria on the right.

"She's also in the orchestra," Henry added.

"Oboe," Heather said making herself comfortable in the chair. "But he often has the blonde play instead of me because she's cheaper for that."

Suddenly Henry tapped his pencil on his notepad. "Kerry, how is the party planning coming for the season announcement."

"We've got about 200 already registered to attend. I've got Janet doing the cooking and we need to go over the menu," Kerry raised a page out of her notebook showing him what he should be looking at.

"Can you email me what Chef Janet thinks is the best?" Henry asked fumbling through his notebook to find the correct page. Once he found the page labeled menu, he pulled it out.

"I will do that. From what I recall, we have several different options," Kerry pointed to the menu page. "She was thinking salmon."

"Roast beef," Jana stressed with a louder tone. "Carving table is a must. Not everyone likes fish or pork, for goodness' sake."

Maria couldn't help but glance back over to Henry Coggins. He noticed her looking back and smiled at her.

"So, what do you think, Maria? Roast beef or salmon?" The conductor asked her with his grin widening.

She didn't realize he was talking to her as she stared back. He quickly chuckled. "I take that as Maria can't decide. Truly, Kerry, with all that's on my plate, I could care less with these details, but I tend to agree that roast beef is a favorite."

Heather nodded, her hair shimmering with different colors. "Roast beef it is."

Maria was still staring at him. He glanced back at her. For a moment, they sat looking at one another until Jana coughed to interrupt.

"So, I was thinking that we should do an outside billboard for the Christmas concert," Jana said.

"Whatever you think," Henry didn't move his eyes from Maria's.

"It will cost a million dollars," Jana said matter-of-factly.

"A million is fine," he mumbled, as if in a trance.

"Oh, boy, and you can buy me a Corvette," Jana added with hope.

"Sure." Henry then leaned over to Maria. "There is this function to raise scholarship money for local college music students. It would be an appropriate place for you to start taking photos. It's this Friday at 8 in the village."

"I think I can make it," Maria gasped, starting to blush.

"And you can buy me a fur coat, too," Jana said.

Suddenly, Henry Coggins straightened and turned to Jana. "A fur coat! Have you gone mad, woman? That's profit for poachers!"

"At least I was paying attention during the meeting," she then whispered, "Flirt."

"If you all will excuse me. I really do have to get to another meeting," Henry Coggins stood, glanced at Maria one last time. "I will see you Friday. The rest of you next month. Have a great day."

CHAPTER 7

I watched Jana Mires walk down the stairs in front of me. She was wearing high heels that matched the color of her moss-green dress. Even in stilettoes, she managed to step downstairs with grace and ease. It was all I could do not to stomp behind her gripping the rail. Jana and I were first to leave the meeting, and at the bottom of the stairs, Jennifer Miller sat behind the desk.

"Jana," she greeted with a smile.

"So nice to see you again, Jenny," Jana said softly with a twist of her golden blonde hair.

Jana walked past her and out the door.

"It's like watching a model, isn't it?" Jennifer snipped, shuffling the papers on her desk. "At least her perfume doesn't stink like Bartwell's."

"That is kind of strong lavender," I squinted my nose. "Smells expensive."

"Only the strongest lavender perfume on the planet our cellist wears," Jennifer said, straightening her frame. "Gives me a headache."

"I have allergies, too," I admitted, sniffling.

The phone suddenly rang; Jennifer answered immediately, "Palms Symphony Orchestra, how can I help you?"

I couldn't hear the other end of the conversation, but a look of sheer horror rolled across Jennifer's face. "All right, you can pick it up as soon as possible. *Chaminade, Flute Concertino in D. Major.* Got it!"

"Is everything okay?" My eyes widened as she ended the conversation.

Jennifer winced and frowned. "I forgot to mail out a piece of music to our flautist who has a recital. That means I better haul ass into the library before she gets here. Her panties are in a wad."

Jennifer was very down to earth, which made me feel comfortable. I liked her immediately and especially that she kept her hair gray. She didn't feel the need to dye it even though she looked to be in her forties.

Jennifer rose from her chair and padded to the music library door. She pulled out a key from her pocket and went in. I stood in the doorway, shocked at how long the hall continued and filled with file cabinet after file cabinet. There must be thousands of pieces of music.

"I'll just be a minute. Don't scare me!" Jennifer roared as she went to the Cabinet marked C and fumbled through the files. "Just a minute. I promise then I'll be out your way."

"Who are you talking to?" I asked matter-of-factly.

"The spirit," Jennifer said, finding the music and shutting the cabinet door. "The ghost leaves me alone if I explain what I am doing and that I will not be there long."

I grinned, raising a brow. "You believe that there's a ghost in there?"

Jennifer rushed to the door clutching a piece of music titled *Chaminade, Flute Concertino in D.* "Don't say things like that," Jennifer said. "I don't mean to be rude, but that angers it when you don't believe."

"Okay, okay," I waved approvingly, "I don't want to stress you out."

Suddenly, a loud crash came from the back of the music library.

"What the heck was that?" I glanced down the hallway toward the cabinets and saw a bust of Mozart lying on the floor.

"That was the ghost's way of saying our flautist should play *Mozart's Concerto No. 1* instead of *Chaminade*."

My eyes tightened in disbelief. "Really? Now the ghost demands what pieces of music the musicians should play?"

Jennifer's face seemed to curl into a smile. "I'm sorry. That sounded crazy, didn't it?" Jennifer rushed to the back of the hall, lifted the bust of Mozart and placed it back on top of the filing cabinet. "She asked for this piece for her recital coming up! Not Mozart. I know you prefer Mozart, but you have got to let this go."

I concluded that Jennifer must have mental issues, so I waited until Jennifer left the music library and locked the door. "Does this ghost have a name?"

"No," Jennifer admitted as she sat back down with the flute music. "We don't have a clue. Scares me every time. Thinking about calling one of those paranormal experts in or clergy to cleanse the room."

My hand went to her shoulder to comfort her. "Have you talked to a counselor about this?"

"Didn't you just see that statue fall off the filing cabinet?" Jennifer glanced at me with disbelief. "I'm not making this up."

"When you closed the filing cabinet, it shook the others and the bust fell. There's a rational explanation."

Jennifer's eyes filled with tears, wanting me to believe. "Everyone thinks I am making this up, but I swear there is something in there and I have to protect people from whatever it is."

Quietly, we left the library. Suddenly, Kerry Bartwell padded down the stairs. The smell of lavender perfume made me sneeze and she changed the subject.

"That was a great meeting. I'll call Janet to set up the food for the party." Kerry said, looking at me. "Henry sure took a liking to you." With that, she quickly existed.

"That stinks so bad," Jennifer said, raising a finger to her nose. "Probably expensive."

I sneezed again.

"There's Kleenex on my desk," Jennifer pointed.

Before I could sneeze again, she rushed for a piece of tissue to cover her nose. Then she folded it and tossed it in the trash can.

"I'm off to do laundry," I admitted, heading towards the door. "Hope you are okay, Jennifer."

"I'm fine," Jennifer said, slightly lowering her tone. "Nothing to worry about probably just my imagination."

CHAPTER 8

Henry Coggins didn't get far. As I hurried from the office building, I found the conductor talking to a man in a black Lexus convertible sports car. The top was down, and Henry was leaning over, talking to him. It didn't take me but a moment to recognize who was driving. I rushed over and interrupted. "There you are. I have called you half a dozen times and you never call me back."

The man behind the wheel took off his sunglasses and revealed brilliant blue eyes. "Is that the way to talk to your brother?" he said.

"Donnie, I am sick of you worrying Mom like this. How long as it been since you contacted either of us," I snipped.

Suddenly, Henry placed his hand on my shoulder. The feel of his hand stopped my anger immediately and I glanced up to notice the very handsome man smiling down at me.

"I've been a little busy with a new case," Donnie said.

"That's more important than worrying your mother and me?" I frowned.

Henry lowered his hand down my back. The very feeling of Henry's fingers on me sent chills down my spine, but I quickly looked away from his brilliant smile to glare back at my younger sibling.

"It is a serious case involving a family member of a famous singer. He's performing at Pulse Nightclub in Orlando, so I am going there tonight, and I promise I'll call you tomorrow."

"Promise?" I gasped, folding my arms.

"Yes," he shifted his sunglasses back on his nose.

"How do you two know each other?" I questioned, glancing back up to Henry's handsome face.

Henry Coggins shifted on his feet. "Your brother represented the orchestra in a lawsuit involving a fall at one of our concerts. He did an excellent job of proving that the woman has had four other cases involving falls."

I lowered my gaze to my brother. "I see. So, you got me this job, Donnie?"

"Whoa, Sis! I just told my friend Henry that my sister is very good at social media and that you recently lost your husband and could use a job, although she has yet to find anyone to date on Matchdot.com," he laughed, grabbing his belly.

I pursed my lip and then gazed up at Henry Coggins. He seemed amused by the argument. "Are you going somewhere, Maestro?"

"Yes, I am late for a meeting, but I think I'd better stay here and protect my attorney from his sister," he laughed.

"I don't mean to bring you into my family problems," I said, grimacing.

"There are no problems," Donnie disagreed, touching the wheel. "It's just that I am a very busy and don't have time to babysit."

"Babysit?" I gasped.

Henry removed his hand and took a step back. "I am out

of this round."

"I am not the one who won't return phone calls. When was the last time you came to see Mom? She has been worried sick, Donnie. You are horrible about returning phone calls, and you don't say anything even when you do." I stomped my foot.

Donnie got out of the car and opened his arms. "Hug?"

I snipped. "You know that's not fair," but we hugged anyway.

"Okay, so I've been a jerk lately. I've been very busy with this new case." Donnie explained, releasing me and re-entering his vehicle.

"New boyfriend?" I asked. "I haven't even met him yet."

"Oh, you haven't met Joe?" Henry asked inquisitively.

"He knows!" I pouted. "My new boss knows your new boyfriend, but your own sister hasn't a clue about what is happening in your life these days."

"Please calm down, Sis," Donnie said, restarting the convertible.

"Your gay brother is fascinating," Henry commented with a grin.

"Are you…" I almost asked about his sexual orientation and realized how inappropriate it was to ask such a personal question of my employer.

"Gay? No," Henry chuckled. "Do you want me to prove it to you?"

I blushed immediately.

Donnie laughed, replacing his hands on the wheel. "Oh, I knew the second he saw you. This could be a wonderful match."

"What?" I gasped, embarrassed. "Please forgive my brother, Mr. Coggins. He really can be a jerk sometimes."

Donnie nodded. "Henry is a wonderful guy. You two would make a great team even if you never dated each other. You are awesome on social media, Sis, and Henry is trying to start a free concert series. I know how much you like working with the less fortunate."

"The series still has to be approved by the board," Henry reminded, leaning forward.

"Why wouldn't they approve such a good cause?" Donnie asked, raising his hand.

"My average concert can cost as much as $40,000 between the copyrights and the musicians. It would take a lot out of the orchestra's savings every year, and they are worried we won't recover if the sold-out concerts don't continue."

"I see," Donnie huffed. "Only time will tell on that."

"It's a risk the board doesn't want to take," Henry said, stepping back. "However, I really do want to pursue the series and get any of the public who can't afford our average ticket prices to have an opportunity."

"See, Sis," Donnie clicked his seatbelt in place. "He's a Prince of Music."

"I bet he calls his mother," I snipped.

Donnie chuckled. "Okay, I will call Mom tomorrow. Now I've got to get to Orlando. We'll talk then." With that he started the engine and waved goodbye.

Henry leaned down and whispered, "I call her several times a week," then he kissed my cheek and walked toward his large black Hummer.

My hand flew to my cheek, in shock of the warm, comforting touch from his lips.

CHAPTER 9

Jennifer was lying in her four-poster-sized bed, snoring into her Snoopy sheets, when her cell phone woke her suddenly. She rolled over and grabbed the phone next to her from the bamboo and glass side table. "This better be important," Jennifer grumbled into the phone in her large square bedroom which desperately needed dusting.

"This is the Sheriff. We got a call from your security company that there might be a break-in at your office building. They reported that you live nearby and have a key. We are headed to the location now and request the key. Otherwise, our officers will break down the door to arrest the trespasser."

Jenny quickly sat up, lowering her blanket. "Oh my! I'll be right down there."

She jumped off her bed and dragged on a pair of jeans and a T-shirt.

"Who was that?" her husband mumbled as he rolled over to face her from underneath the covers.

"The police. There is a break-in at the PSO office. I have to bring the key or they will break down the door!" Jenny alerted while grabbing her purse.

Before he could even ask, "You want me to go with you?" Jennifer was out the door and darting to her car. She quickly started the engine and raced down a few blocks until she got to the office building by the river. Two police cars were out in front with lights flashing and the building alarm had been triggered. Two officers had flashlights at the door.

Jenny parked and hurried to where the officers were standing. She handed one the key to open the door and enter.

"Thank you," he said, putting the key in the door. "We circled the building and didn't see anything and didn't want to break down your door if the perpetrator already left the scene."

"There is a safe in the music library with the ticket money from our last concert." Jenny alerted, her eyes widening. "It's the room at the bottom of the stairs. Here's the key to that."

The officer opened the front door and then his fingers encircled the smaller library key. "Anything else?"

"Sheet music that's worth thousands and thousands of dollars," Jenny anxiously pressed.

"Wait over there," the Officer pointed to her car. "We'll come get you when we are done searching the area."

"Of course," Jenny said, then returned to her car.

The officers entered; she saw their flashlights slowly going upstairs through the window. Room by room, they searched. Jenny was breathing hard and caught a look at herself in the rearview mirror. Her grey bobbed hair needed to be brushed, and her deep-set green eyes had bags from being woken up so suddenly. "Please, no music stolen," she murmured.

The light was coming from the music library; then she saw the leading overhead light come on. She hoped the ghost would be quiet for the police. Again, she suddenly caught a glimpse of herself in the rearview mirror. Her hair looked like it had a mind of its own. "Eh, you're a sight," she mumbled, trying to brush her hair with her fingers.

The two police officers left the building and approached Jenny's car, so she rolled down the window.

"There's nobody here. It must have been an animal or something on the window. Surprised, the alarm went off, though. The safe looks fine and the library door was locked without any signs of forced entry."

"I see," Jenny for a second got angry. "Just the ghost."

One officer laughed, extending his hand with her keys. "False alarm, Miss. Here are your keys back. We shut off all the lights."

Jenny could see that a light had just come back on. The reflected circle of light on the parking lot made the two officers turn around.

"Didn't you just shut that off?" one officer asked the other.

"Yes, I did and that's coming where the safe would be," he alerted. "Do you have any problems with your electricity?"

Jennifer answered honestly, "Just some flickering lights sometimes."

The officer quickly grabbed the keys out of Jennifer's hand, "We better recheck the library."

The two jogged back to the building; their hands were on their guns.

Jennifer shook her head and said with frustration. "Now the damn thing is calling the cops."

She looked at the door and saw the two officers running

out of the building. Jenny got out of their car and the officer handed her the keys back.

"Not the type of intruder we deal with," he muttered with a flicker of fear in his eyes.

"You weren't lying about the ghost," the other said. "Have a nice night, Miss. There's nothing we can do. No human intruders and nothing stolen." With that, the two officers shuffled to their vehicles and drove off.

Jennifer watched the lights coming on and off in what would be the music library. She had had enough! She was tired of this ghost controlling so much of her life and scaring police officers, even getting her out of bed at two o'clock in the morning. That was it!

Then , she went to the door, unlocked it, and walked right up to the music library door. Before she could put her key in the door, it opened. Suddenly, chills crawled up her spine.

Inside, she could see that nothing was amiss. Only the light was flickering.

"Why did you bring the police here and wake me up?" The hairs on the back of her arms stood up.

Suddenly, a ball of light appeared in the back of the room, about the size of a baseball. Jenny couldn't take her eyes off it. Slowly, it flew across the room and went to the radio on top of one of the filing cabinets. It came on and scrolled across several stations until it stopped on a news report. Several minutes of shock flew past as Jenny finally heard the disturbing report about the Pulse nightclub in Orlando. Several people had been killed at the scene, according to the announcer.

"Oh my!" Jenny gasped in shock. "How horrible!"

Then the light appeared again from the radio, and everything went dark, including the room. Jenny gathered her senses. She flew to the door she locked from the outside, then darted out the front door.

She picked up her phone and scrolled down until she reached Henry Coggins phone. "I bet someone from the orchestra is at Pulse," she surmised. "Our symphony ghost wouldn't be so upset otherwise."

Henry didn't answer.

CHAPTER 10

I couldn't believe someone was pounding on my door at 2:20 in the morning. I thought it wasn't just a slight tap but an impatient bang that could have woken the dead.

My mother had her Tom Jones bathrobe on and was already walking to the door as I rushed to gather a sheet around myself. "Who is it?" Mother asked, peering into the peephole in the front door. "You better stop that banging! We'll call the police, and we got an attack dog here."

Picking up the dog made of bamboo sticks and rope, which was part of the condo decor, I added, "You mean this, Mom."

"Put that down. I just dusted it," Mother snipped, taking the fake dog out of my hands. "Who do you think could be banging on the door at this hour? Can you see who it is from the peephole?"

"I'm sorry to bother you, but this is Henry Coggins!" came a yell through the door. "I am Maria's boss. At least one of her bosses and I am friends with Donnie."

I gasped as she quickly opened the door. Henry started to speak; then his gaze dropped down to my sheet-wrapped body. I looked down and responded, "It's the middle of the night. I was fast asleep. What do you want?"

"Yes, I know." but he didn't take his eyes off of me.

"Does the Palm Orchestra have a social media emergency?" I asked him, watching my mother put the fake dog back on the floor.

"Actually," Henry showed her his phone. I read the text sent from my brother's phone over her shoulder.

"This is from Donnie," I started to read.

"He's in trouble," Henry said, giving me his phone. "I came as soon as I got it. I already called the police. They are already there."

"Police?" Mother asked now, trying to peer over my shoulder at the phone again. "What's all this about? Why are you so upset…is Donnie drunk again?"

I read the text out loud. "Got shot at Pulse. Gunman killing everyone. My client is dead. Tell my family I love them."

"This is some kind of joke," Mom said, stepping back. "Donnie's drinking again. He's imagining things."

"Just turn on the television," Henry said, his voice shaking. "This is no joke. There was a shooting at the Pulse nightclub in Orlando, which is national news. Lots of people have been shot. I can hardly believe it. Do you want a ride to Orlando? The police said they are taking victims to the nearest hospitals. I think Florida Hospital?"

I nearly fainted. Henry grabbed me, and my sheet fell to the ground. There I stood, naked and trembling. My mother quickly grabbed the sheet and put it across my chest and around my bottom.

"Maria, get dressed!" Mother admonished, rushing toward her bedroom. "Hurry!"

I was shaking, but somehow, I hurried to an adjoining room, dragged on a pair of jeans, and popped on a tank top.

I grabbed my purse, and Henry had his Hummer in the driveway waiting when she reached the door. My mother was struggling to get up in the back seat. She used the step and then scooted over in the back so I could take the passenger's side.

I jumped up into the large front seat of the truck and then meekly said, "Thank you for letting us know right away."

"Believe me, the text woke me up, and I thought he was drunk, too, until I turned on the news I realized Donnie was shot!"

I started to cry. "Oh my God. Why Donnie?"

Henry reached out and touched my shoulder. "Now let's not think the worst case here."

"Pulse nightclub?" her mother asked Henry.

"Yes, Ma'am, it was Latin night."

"The shooter was…oh, it's probably a hate crime," Mother shook her head and leaned in a little between the two front seats. "I told my boy not to hang out where bigots could harm him."

"I can't believe it," I wiped my tears, but more cascaded.

"ISIS, I bet," her mother added.

"You think it's a terrorist attack!" I gasped, glancing back at her.

"Terrorist!" Henry agreed as he rubbed Maria's shoulder. "ISIS, maybe. The newscast didn't say it was even a gay nightclub. It's like the news is hiding that."

"Can't you drive any faster?" I gasped as the black Hummer entered the I-95 Highway ramp.

"I will get you there as fast as I can," Henry promised, gripping the wheel.

"How could this happen in America?" Mother asked softly. "This is the 21ˢᵗ century, for goodness sake. Haven't we all done away with hate?"

"SWAT is already there," Henry said. "Whoever did this won't get away with the shooting! First, that female singer was shot. I think she was Donnie's client."

"Oh, yeah," her mother remembered, "the singer from that television show. She was so good."

"Now this!" I gasped.

"Terrible things happen in threes," Henry Coggins said. "My mother always says that to me."

"My Uncle always says that, too," I stated, nodding.

"Let's hope that our suspicions are wrong this time," Henry said, touching me again on the shoulder.

I clasped my hands in prayer. "God, please let my brother be okay. He's way too young to die."

"Yes, Lord, please!" Mother begged. "Help my Donnie!"

Henry Coggins removed his hand from my shoulder and turned the wheel to pass another car on the highway. From then on, no one spoke, not until we pulled up around the block from the Pulse nightclub in Orlando into a living nightmare.

CHAPTER 11

"I'll see what I can find out," Henry said, getting out of the truck. He walked over to a police officer in the middle of the street. They shared words, but Maria couldn't help but see the dead bodies outside the club.

"This is still happening," Maria murmured to her mother.

"There are dead bodies over there," her mother gasped, staring at the twisted bodies covered in blood. "Please don't let my boy be dead."

Suddenly, Henry rushed back behind the wheel, stepping over another motionless body. The smell of blood flooded in when he opened the door. Sirens were deafening. "Several of the wounded have been taken to Florida Hospital. "Let's go there. He said the gunman has been killed, but about fifty people didn't make it. See if we can find Donnie."

"Oh no!" Maria cried out.

Henry started the truck to begin heading toward the hospital. The traffic was heavy with so many bringing the injured to the hospital; there were not enough ambulances. Maria couldn't help but cry. Her mother reached around the seat and put her hand on her arm in comfort.

The moment they pulled in front of the busy hospital, Henry parked, and the three rushed toward the doors. Inside, people were bleeding and being attended to.

"Excuse me," Henry asked a nurse bandaging a man's bleeding arm. "We are looking for someone who was at Pulse. Do you have the names of the people brought here?"

"Are you family?"

"Yes, they are," Henry pointed to Maria and her mom. "His name is Donnie Wilson and he's about six foot and has brown hair."

The nurse checked that her bandage was tight and then stood. "Speak to the woman at that desk. She can help you."

Henry rushed over and asked. "Do you have a Donnie Wilson here?"

The woman fumbled through some papers on a clipboard, "Not all the victims are here. They are also at Memorial Hospital a few miles away." She looked hurried.

An ambulance with blaring sirens suddenly pulled up and two EMTs rushed in pulling a man on a cot. He was covered in blood and his face was unrecognizable. But the moment he came into the room, he started shouting. "Mom! Mom, it's me!"

Maria rushed over to the cot and screamed, "Donnie!"

Henry ran to be by her side, "Donnie?"

"It's not my blood," he said as a doctor began to examine him.

"You're alive!" Maria cried out.

"I was shot, but it just grazed my leg. I hid in the bathroom underneath all these corpses," Donnie mumbled. "It was a war zone. The guy was mental. He laughed as he was shooting at everyone!"

Maria hugged him. She didn't care that he was covered in blood. She was so happy that her brother was alive.

"You'll need to talk to the police," the doctor said. "Now show me your wound!"

Donnie's hands went to his right leg. It was completely covered in blood with a rip across the left side of the knee. "The bullet went right through my pant leg," he explained.

The doctor took a pair of scissors and began cutting the jeans up to his knee. Underneath, the skin was not bloody, with only a scratch on the side of the knee. With one hand, the doctor pressed on the wound.

"Move your knee," the doctor ordered. Donnie moved his leg and then let out a yelp.

"You've got a bullet lodged in your knee and need surgery immediately," the doctor announced.

"You're kidding," Donnie said.

"You are pumped up on adrenaline," the doctor added. "You don't feel it."

"It feels like a scratch," Donnie gasped.

"We're going to have to take him to surgery so he won't lose his leg," the doctor told Maria. "He will survive, though, which is much more than I have had to tell about a dozen families already tonight."

Maria suddenly hugged the doctor. "Thank you!"

"I might lose my leg," Donnie said.

"You're alive and in good hands," his mother kissed his bloody cheek. "We'll be right here. We're not leaving you."

The doctor and nurses began pushing Donnie away. "I'll

let you know when he's in recovery," the doctor softly added.

Hours passed, like years. Henry, Maria, and her mom were in the surgery recovery room, waiting and watching the breaking news on television. They were calling the shooter a terrorist. Since Pulse was a gay club on Latino night, it was considered the most heinous of hate crimes, said reporter after reporter.

Henry pulled Maria onto his shoulder. "Donnie is alive. We are fortunate for that."

Maria's Mom raised her hands to pray with a quivering voice, "Dear Lord, help my son keep his leg. Guide the doctors as they operate on him. Be with the families of the victims. Heal this country from hate. Amen."

"Nearly 50 dead," Henry said. "Just because they decided to have a few drinks at a club."

"Is it wrong of me to be so thankful that Donnie is alive when so many are dead right now?" Maria asked him.

Henry smiled. "No, not wrong."

"Selfish of me?" Maria wondered.

"No," Henry said, then leaned down and kissed her forehead.

"Am I awful to think I should be putting this stuff on social media?" Maria asked.

Henry chuckled, "No, it just means I hired the right person.

CHAPTER 12

We waited hours in the operating room with a few couples. The television was blaring all the events happening at the Pulse nightclub. Henry found it odd that they didn't ever mention that it was a gay club or that it was Latin night. The word "Terrorist" came up often as "ISIS."

Sitting and watching the horrific events being telecast only made Maria feel very blessed that her brother was one of the few who made it out alive and that he would be a survivor.

Henry sat next to her, thumbing through *Golf* magazines, but never stayed on a page long enough to read anything. His attention was drawn to the flat screen above us on the opposite wall from the sofas.

"I want to sleep," said her mother. "But I just can't. I worry about Donnie and what's happening in that operation room." Her skin looked pallid under the fluorescent lights; her eyelids drooped.

"How long has it been?" I asked Henry.

He glanced down at his watch. "Five hours. It's been a very long operation. I wonder if I should ask the nurse for an update."

"That's a great idea," her mother thanked him.

Henry rose and went to the nursing station across the hall. Words were exchanged and then Henry came back without any expression across his face. His hands were clasped.

"The doctor is coming to talk to us," Henry announced.

"Is Donnie in the recovery room yet?" her mother asked.

"Yes," Henry said. "They are in the process of that now."

Suddenly, a side door opened, and the same doctor who had quickly wheeled Donnie away walked in. His face looked paler, and he seemed tired. "Good morning," the doctor greeted.

"How is Donnie?" I begged of him.

The Doctor rolled over a chair and sat in front of the group. Henry sat down and put his arm around her. From Henry's movements and the Doctor sitting down at their level, Maria knew something had gone wrong.

"I have some positive news and some that will upset you. If you want, I can give your mother a sedative."

"Oh no! God help us! What happened?"

"Mom, you have Valium in your purse; take one," Maria suggested.

Her mother fumbled through her pocketbook and quickly engulfed a pill. Her hands were shaking while she fought back tears.

"Donnie is alive and in stable condition," the doctor said. "However, we are moving him to ICU for observation for 24-48 hours."

"What's wrong?" her mother questioned.

"The bullet destroyed the knee. When I went it, I discovered it was completely shattered and that the bone below the knee was also in so many pieces that knee replacement wasn't possible."

"Amputation?" Henry asked.

"No!" her mother gasped.

"I am very sorry to report to you to save your son's life and his ability to walk again, I had to remove this leg just above the knee. At first, this news is quite devastating, but with proper care and prosthetics, Donnie will live a full and rich life."

"Like that girl on 'Dancing with the Stars'?" her mother remembered. "She had two fake legs and danced so well!"

"Yes, she nearly won," the doctor smiled as he remembered.

"So, Donnie will wake up and not have a leg?" Henry said.

"Yes, usually it is the doctor who tells the patient, but if you would prefer to be the first one to tell him, I would be okay with that," the doctor said. "To be honest, this is my very first amputee, but I was in conference with an orthopedic surgeon who guided my every move. He felt it was a miracle that your son didn't bleed to death."

"Is he getting blood?" her mother asked.

"Yes, we had to give him an emergency transfusion and luckily, we had enough blood. We are running out and asking the community to donate."

"Where can I donate?" Henry asked immediately.

"There is a Red Bus right out front now," the doctor explained. "It would be great if you donated."

"I will! Whatever I can do to help."

"We are swamped with patients now," the doctor said. "I did all I could to save his leg, but it wasn't even a possibility. I had hoped that a knee replacement would have been possible, but we couldn't get proper measurements, and the bones were just too splintered."

"Thank you for all you have done for my brother," Maria said. "I will tell him about the leg."

"Okay, then, after you have told him. I will come in, and so will a prosthetic advisor so that he will immediately learn that life will be different but that he can do everything he once did before being shot," the doctor gulped. "Now, if you will excuse me. We have dozens of people needing my help now. Donnie will recover for several hours, but I'll have a nurse come and get you as soon as he wakes up. I must warn you of phantom pain and that he may not even realize that his leg is gone until he fully wakes. We have him on some painkillers, but if they are not enough, just let the ICU Floor Nurse know and they can give him an injection to help calm him down."

"Thank you, Doctor," Maria said, her eyes welling with tears.

"Again, I am very sorry I couldn't do more," the doctor said. He nodded to her mother, shook Henry's hand, and quietly plodded out.

CHAPTER 13

An hour passed before a nurse came to escort us to the recovery room. Maria wasn't sure what she would say. She wasn't even sure she could handle seeing her brother Donnie without a leg.

She knew she had to remain strong.

"Do you want me to wait here or come with you?" Henry asked.

Her mother s miled. "Thank you for respecting our privacy but you are more than welcome. I think Maria would be grateful for your support."

Maria tried not to show how upset she was by nodding. "Unless you don't want to come."

"No, I do," Henry said. "Donnie saved the orchestra by handling that slip and fall, and I owe him a lot. We got to know each other, and I like him very much and consider him a friend."

"Not every friend would want to be there in this situation," her mother concluded. "That shows of your character, Mr. Coggins."

"Thank you," he waited until she stood, saw she left her coat on the chair, and helped place it around her shoulders.

"And you are quite a gentleman."

Henry followed the two women who trailed the nurse. The nurse took them up and down several hallways that appeared all the same, only the letters on the signs changed on the walls.

The nurse then faced them. "We have taken him to a private room. The doctor will be alerted of your meeting and will be in shortly with medical care information and a list of rehab facilities in your area."

"Couldn't he stay with us," Maria asked.

"Not for a few weeks to a month," the nurse informed, "but you can visit him often."

"I won't leave his side," said his mother.

The door opened and Donnie was lying in the hospital bed. Surprisingly for Maria, he was not covered in tubes or any oxygen. He seemed peaceful, lying there with a sheet over him. It is evident by the lack of height on one side that the leg was gone but Donnie was snoring and unaware as far as she could tell.

"He's been in and out of consciousness," the nurse reported.

"Maria took the second chair. Her mother took the first closest to him, and Henry stood."

"I'll bring another chair," said the nurse.

"I'm fine," Henry added.

"Please bring one," Maria asked her.

Another hour passed before Donnie opened his eyes. Immediately, her mother held his hand as he woke. "Hello, Son," she whispered.

Donnie smiled, "I made it?"

"Yes, Honey, you are alive, and your family is quite happy about that."

"It was a nightmare," Donnie said. "I was laying under dead bodies, and the guy was nuts. He was laughing as he was killing people."

"I know you have been through a lot," the mother murmured.

"Hey, Henry," Donnie seemed pleased to see him. "Thank you so much for bringing my mom and sister here. You are the best!"

Henry walked over and patted Donnie on the shoulder. "I wouldn't want to be anywhere else, my friend."

"Honey, I have something to tell you, "Her mother added. "There was a complication with the operation and the doctor will be here soon to explain that you will be going into a rehab facility to learn how to walk again."

"I don't need to go to a nursing home," Donnie grimaced.

"It's a rehab center. There is one not even a half mile from our condo and it would be perfect for everyone to visit you as you heal up from…" Before his mother could finish her sentence, Donnie's eyes had moved to what was once his leg. He quickly moved the sheet.

Maria couldn't look at the covered limb. It had blood still on the bandages and immediately showed that it had been cut off.

"My leg!" Donnie cried out. "My leg! It's gone! Oh no!

No, I thought the doctor would try to save it."

"You'll get a prosthetic limb," Maria started to cry. "You're still alive."

"Am I?" Donnie looked as if in shock. "I can't even believe what I've seen and now this. All those people are dead. All of them are so young! He just kept shooting, and people were screaming and begging for their lives. How could anyone be so cruel? I have represented some pretty bad characters, drug addicts, prostitutes, even those I knew weren't as injured as they claimed, but this man was an evil I have never seen before. He wanted to kill us all."

"You are alive," Maria whispered. "Yes, your life will be different but in time you will be able to do everything you did before. There are people in prosthetics who jog and dance."

"I'll never be able to play tennis again," Donnie's eyes welled up.

"Well, you weren't that good at it anyway," Henry smiled. "I beat you every time, and your swing was all wrong."

Suddenly, Donnie laughed through the tears. "You are right. I wasn't very good at it and to be honest, I wouldn't say I like tennis. I prefer jogging."

"You'll be able to do that with a prosthetic," said his mother," her mother said. "And you can still give your mother a big hug." She stood and leaned over her son. They held each other as he cried onto her shoulder.

"Why me?" Donnie said. "Why am I alive? Why did all this happen? Was he a terrorist? Why did he do this? Was it because it was a gay bar? Did he hate Latinos? Why did this monster do this?"

"Did you see the police kill him?" Maria asked.

"No, I was hiding in the bathroom. The ladies' bathroom at that. I just ran and hid under all these women who were dying and shot." Henry wiped his eyes. "I can't even talk about it."

Then the door opened, and in walked the doctor. He was carrying a folder and a handful of papers he gave Maria. "These are some things to look over, and when Donnie is ready you can let him have them. Anesthesia lasts about 24 hours, so let's wait until after that time."

CHAPTER 14

The doctor began to talk to Donnie. Donnie started to cry as we listened. The doctor voiced suggestions about rehabilitation and prosthetics while Donnie called openly.

There had only been a few times in my life that I remember Donnie crying so hard. Once, when we were on the playground and my mom had thought he was in the car. At the last minute, he remembered that he had left his stuffed bear on the bench right outside the swing sets. He jumped out and ran toward the brown bear with the blue tie. Mom hadn't noticed that he had gotten out or heard him say, "Left Teddy," since the radio was on. For some reason, I didn't say anything. I just watched as Mom drove off.

Mom checked the backseat about a mile away, "Where's Donnie?" she asked me.

A part of me wondered if I should tell her. He had pulled my ponytail all morning and tossed sand in my face in the playground. "At the park," I finally murmured.

I'd never seen anyone drive as fast as we did that day. When we pulled in Donnie was on the ground bawling his eyes out, cuddling that bear, like it was the only thing on earth that loved him.

Mom rushed out and held him so tight. At the time, I smiled. Maybe I wasn't always the best sister. Even then, I was jealous of the attention that Mom was giving my brother; I felt jealous but also sorry for not saying anything sooner.

The next time I saw him cry was at Dad's funeral. Even

though our parents divorced, Donnie was always so close to Dad who died from lung cancer, and I believe it was then that Donnie decided to become a lawyer and fight Big Tobacco.

This time when Donnie cried, he continued to listen to the doctor. Henry was standing beside him with his hand on his shoulder. Donnie and Henry seemed like good friends. Donnie had many straight friends, so I wasn't surprised by the friendship, only that the man I had heard was difficult to get to know was very empathetic.

The doctor made everything seem like this was just a bump in the road and that Donnie would resume his normal life soon after rehab. Donnie seemed to take the news as well as anyone could.

"Why does it feel like my leg is still there?" Donnie asked.

"Are you in pain?"

"It doesn't feel good," Donnie said.

"We'll adjust your pain medicine," then the doctor explained phantom pain and its causes.

"Do you have any questions for me?" the doctor asked Donnie.

Donnie didn't seem to have any. "Not at this time."

"You can cross-examine me later," the doctor shook his hand. "We'll release you in a few days and send you to the rehab facility you pick."

"Thank you," Donnie said.

The moment the doctor left. "I would like to be alone for a while. I realize you all drove all this way, but I will go to

Sunrise Rehab, and we can visit a lot then."

"I don't want to leave," Mom said.

"I need some time to accept this," Donnie said.

"Are you sure?" Henry asked.

"We can get a hotel room, Donnie," I suggested. "You might want to see us later."

"No, go home, and I'll take a courtesy van."

"Out of the question," Mom said. "We will stay in Orlando and go with you. You are not going through this alone."

After Mom spoke, that was the end of that conversation. Donnie realized we would not leave him in Orlando while he was going through all this, mainly because there could be complications."

Henry said, "I have nothing on my books for a few days."

"You want to stay too?" I asked him.

"Yes," Henry said. "In fact, why don't we give Donnie some time and get a few rooms at a hotel nearby."

"We'll be back later tonight," her mother said.

Then I leaned over and kissed my brother on the forehead. "Everything will be all right," I promised him.

"I certainly won't be as frightening in the courtroom."

"That's not true," Henry said. "If anyone even notices that you are wearing a prosthetic leg, then they will realize you are a fighter and that nothing will stop you. Not even on one leg will you ever lose your cases. I've seen you in the courtroom. I know what you can do, and that won't end with one leg."

"You're right. My mouth still works," Donnie smiled.

"The pain will get better," Mom said, kissing his cheek, "with time."

"Okay, I'll see you guys later," Donnie wiped his eyes. "You have no idea of what I have been through. I will never get over what happened at Pulse."

Henry shook his hand and then escorted us to the door. "I'll get them a hotel room and myself one. We'll be back in a few hours. We all need some rest and time to digest what has happened."

"Thank you, Henry, for helping."

"Anytime."

"Bye," I said to my brother. For some reason, this felt very different from when we were kids and when we left him at the park.

This time, I wanted to get his teddy bear for him.

CHAPTER 15

"Thank you, Heather, for coming to the office tonight," Jenny said, opening the door. "So glad you were available and not working on the graphics tonight.

"The graphics for the next concert can wait until the morning." Heather shook her head and her multi-colored hair moved ever so slightly as she entered the office carrying a brown duffle bag. "I had heard rumors that we might have a ghost in the office, but I didn't want to say anything. When you talk about this kind of stuff, people think you're off putting."

"To be honest, no one believes me," Jenny said, relocking the door behind Heather. "After what happened last night,, I became worried that the ghost had started to become violent or take a turn for the worse."

Jenny suddenly shivered. "You see what I mean? There's a heaviness and chill in the office now."

Heather entered and placed her duffle bag and purse on Jenny's desk. "I'm glad you called me."

"I had heard that you dabbled in the paranormal when you're not creating art." Jenny glanced over to the music library door.

"I do," Heather unzipped her bag and pulled out a small handheld box, "This is an EMF detector. It will light up if there is a ghost present. I also have a Voice Recorder to catch any disembodied voices."

"It doesn't speak," Jenny questioned as she examined the

box. "At least I've never heard it."

"It might be demonic, then. Does it make noises like grunting?" Heather moved toward the music library door.

Jenny took out her key to open the music library. "No, it's human because it wrote on the ceiling."

"It wrote on the ceiling?" Heather gasped as her eyes widened. "I need to get my whole Ghost Hunting Group to this location and document all of this."

Jenny turned around and faced the PSO Graphic Artist with blue and purple hair. "No, Heather. We need to keep this under wraps for the sake of the orchestra. Henry will get angry otherwise, and he has enough on his plate right now with all that's happened in Orlando. Maria's brother was there, got shot, and lost his leg. He's that lawyer friend that helped the symphony, remember?"

"Dwight?"

"No, Donnie Wilson," Jenny corrected as she unlocked the library door. "The conductor will be away for a few more days but has to return for that college music fundraiser. He's already committed to be a speaker. We don't need this kind of media attention or any volunteer loss."

"Okay, can I at least bring my paranormal group here to do a full investigation? We won't tell anyone." Heather promised, looking into the room full of filing cabinets along both walls.

"Can we trust them?" Jenny sounded doubtful.

"Yes, we will keep it hush. We do that a lot when children are involved. We had this one case in which we thought a demon was possessing a nine-year-old. We had to call in a priest, but we finally did get rid of it." Heather slowly stepped into the music library.

"I don't want to know about those sorts of things, "Jenny investigated the music library and followed Heather. "What!"

Heather looked up to the ceiling. "There's nothing. Didn't you say it was written in blood?"

"It's gone. The words, 'I am here.' Gone!" Jenny gasped as she stared up to the white popcorn ceiling.

"How could you!" Jenny suddenly screamed at the ceiling. "Why did you write words and then take them down?"

Heather patted her shoulder as she took a deep breath. "Those words may have only been for you, then."

"It got me here and told me what was happening by turning on the radio in Orlando. It wanted me to know that the flautist picked the wrong music, too. This thing communicates with me, but only me!" Jenny sounded panicked. Her face flushed as her breathing sped up.

Heather removed her hand and showed that the voice recorder was in her hand. "Let's see about that."

"Please, this isn't my imagination. There's something here. I know everyone thinks I am making it up so no one comes in here." Jenny pushed a large painting on the wall to the side. It was of Henry Coggins conducting with swirling lines as if he had superpowers as he worked. There was the artist's signature in the corner. "See, there's a safe in here. But that isn't the reason."

"Is that where the ticket money is kept?" Heather

questioned, examining the safe.

"Yes, from those that come in to buy tickets, but this is mostly from donations mailed in. I keep the money here until I go to the bank twice a month." Jenny explained, opening a box full of checks, some cash. She then shut the box and slammed the safe door shut.

"So, there's a lot of value in there." Heather gulped.

"Sometimes a hundred thousand or more…" Jenny alerted as she hung the painting back in place. "That's why when our security alarm went off, I rushed down here as soon as possible. I live only a few blocks away. The police came and searched the entire building. Then they saw the letters and ran. At least that's what I think they saw anyway. They didn't really say. They just left in a hurry and said that they don't deal with this kind of problem."

"No, they haven't been trained to handle the paranormal but let's see. Car accidents and other sudden deaths often cause them to cross paths with ghosts. They don't talk about it much. My group wanted to do a lecture for the first responders, but the sheriff practically laughed us out of the station."

"I know what no one believing you feels like," Jenny's eyes watered as she stepped away from the painting to make sure it was level.

Heather reached out and patted her arm. "I'm going to help you prove it's here. Maybe find some answers too."

"Thank you," Jenny started to cry. "I'm at my wit's end. Even my husband thinks I need to see a doctor."

Heather turned on the recorder. "Hello, my name is Heather, and I am the graphic artist for the symphony. I am with Jenny who you keep showing yourself to. We want to know what you want. What is your name? Why are you here?"

She waited a few moments.

"That's all there is too it?" Jenny asked.

"Sometimes you can hear a disembodied voice when you play it back."

"Tell us your name, please!" Heather said as clearly as possible and slowly. "Your name! Please tell us your name! Did you ever walk the earth? Were you human?" Silence again.

A few more minutes passed as the voice recorder continued to record. Then Heather pressed stopped and played it back. They could hear Heather's voice. "Did you ever walk the earth? Were you human?"

A second or two she was passed on the tape. Then suddenly, like a whisper, a man's voice was heard. "Yes."

CHAPTER 16

We planted ourselves at a hotel just down the road from the hotel. I left Mom and my hotel room number with both Donnie and the floor nurse in case Donnie needed us before tonight.

Henry got a separate adjoining room. Through the walls I could hear him making phone calls about the next upcoming concert. He talked to musicians and stage crew about various necessaries.

He was not what I had expected. Clearly, he was as handsome as everyone had described to her, but he was far different than a Maestro with an attitude. There seemed to be no ego in him; he had a kind and caring heart. Thinking about it, Maria couldn't imagine that many men would have done so much for their company lawyer.

Donnie and Henry seemed to be good friends. It's no wonder why someone like her, with not much social media experience or even marketing experience, landed such an incredible job.

It was easy to see that Donnie had set this up. Perhaps he even thought they would make a great couple. Suddenly laughter came to her lips. He believed that someone with that much fame, money and good looks would date her! Her! Really, she was outclassed and outmatched.

Once Donnie had set her up in high school, she remembered. His name was Danny Hendershop. He was on the football team with him and very good looking. Danny did take her to prom, was a gentleman the entire night, but after that one date never called her again. Oh, and then there was Brian Hines. Hines was also attractive, but he couldn't keep his hands off of her. Donnie made a few anti-gay bigoted comments during the date and that was the last I ever wanted to see of Donnie. He didn't know that my brother was gay but that was still no excuse to be so uneducated and rude.

My mother sat down next to me on the bed. "Do you mind if I close the curtains and get some shut eye?"

"No, not at all."

Suddenly, a knock came at the adjoining door. I got up and answered it. Henry was behind the door fully dressed in a suit.

"I was going downstairs to the dining room. Would you both like to join me?"

"We haven't eaten since dinner last night, Mom. Do you want to go?" I asked her.

"I need to rest. I had some snack food at the hospital. I am fine for now. You two, go, Honey," her mom replied.

"Are you hungry?" he asked me.

I was but for far more than just food. He was about the most handsome man I had ever met. His personality was that of someone she could easily far in love with. She had even been warned not to fall for him.

"Are you?" he repeated, waiting for my answer.

"I'm famished," I announced.

"Good, let's go. I've been to this hotel before, and the food here is fabulous. Although the menu is small, the taste is huge."

"All right," I turned back to my mother. "I'll be back in an hour or so."

"Take your time. I'll be sleeping," her mother said.

"Why don't we pick up one of their sandwiches and put it in the fridge for her to eat whenever she wants," Henry suggested.

"Great idea," her mother began shutting the hotel curtains.

Maria took several steps forward into Henry's hotel room. She shut the adjoining door between them and followed him to the door. He glanced back at her and smiled just as he opened the door for her.

"You are quite the gentlemen," Maria said. "I can't thank you enough for all that you have done to help my family."

"You are taking Donnie, losing his leg pretty hard," Henry commented as they stepped inside the hotel elevator.

"How else am I supposed to take this? This is a nightmare."

"All those people dead." Henry sighed heavily. "It's hard to even conceive of the horror they saw, what your brother saw. I was glad to hear that the rehab facility where he'll live also has counselors on staff."

"Donnie will certainly need that," Maria said.

"You might, too. There is no shame in asking for help or talking about things that concern you. This horrific act of terror will affect many people in many ways. So, if you need counseling, I can talk to our insurance company and make sure you get any treatment you may need."

"You aren't what I expected, Mr. Coggins," Maria said.

"Thank you," Henry smiled. "The last person to tell me that was at the last board meeting. I've been trying to get a free series of concerts available throughout the year, patriotic, Christmas and Easter."

"Free?" Maria raised a brow.

"Yes, I know that sounds a bit odd coming from a man whose company normally charges a hundred dollars a ticket, but there is a real need in this community for the elderly, military, and the young. We can't expect to encourage our youth to become musicians when the only way they can see our concerts is on television or on their iPhone."

Maria nodded. "I agree."

"I didn't come from money," Henry said. "My Mom worked two jobs just so that I could have music lessons."

"What did you play?" Maria wondered.

"The French Horn. I am what you may have heard called a Band Geek. I grew up barely able to afford my lessons. My music teacher made a deal with my mother many times that if she sewed up some dresses for his daughters, he would not charge for a month of lessons. He even provided the materials for the clothing."

"He must have seen something in you," Maria said.

"I am a much better conductor than a musician," Henry said. "but I love music. Music has always been my best friend."

"Funny you should say that" Maria said. "That's how I

feel when I sing gospel music at my church. I find that it brings me closer to God."

Henry just looked at her for a moment. Then suddenly, he reached out and held her hand. "You are quite beautiful, Maria."

Maria glanced down, trying desperately not to tell him that if he didn't stop saying things like that, she would fall madly in love.

CHAPTER 17

"Don't you write music as well," Maria asked. "I think I had read that somewhere in the paper."

Henry smiled, "Composition is a great love of mine. I wrote a piece not long ago that the symphony played, and then a friend of mine, another Maestro in North Carolina had his orchestra play it too. So far, it's been very well received, and I just signed the contract to have it published."

"Congrats," Maria tightened the hold on his hand. "That must bring you so much joy to hear something that you have written played."

"A feeling I can't even describe. You know it's ironic. I conduct hundreds of pieces of music a year but the one I wrote made me a basket-case. I was so nervous I nearly vomited. No kidding."

"I can understand that," Maria smiled.

"It had this incredible violin solo entrance with a very harmonic melody. The motif is quite unforgettable. I named the piece, "Buttercup.""

Maria laughed, "Like the flower or a lover's nickname."

"No," Henry said. "It is named after the world's most beautiful violin. The one owned by my Concertmaster Hiroki."

"Yes, I have heard of that violin. It is worth millions."

"One of the most valuable violins in the world," Henry

admitted, "many of our patrons come just to see it and hear Hiroki play."

"You must be very proud then."

"To have Hiroki as my Concertmaster is quite an honor. He is quite famous worldwide, and the sound of his Stradivarius is one that most people never get the honor of hearing and I enjoy every week."

"What does he think of your free concert idea?" Maria wondered.

"He wouldn't have to do them if he didn't want to. I have several violinists who could step in if necessary. His contract is only for the PSO classical series. My idea would bring in a more modern concert series called "Pops.""

"And this series would be open to the public?"

"Yes, free and with open seating so those who normally can only afford to sit in the nose-bleed section of the auditorium can now sit in the front row and smell my sweat," Henry laughed.

"This means a lot to you. I can see that."

"It me, it is at the very core of what I want to accomplish. Music is for everyone, not just the rich. That also brings me to my next idea of allowing those who can't afford tickets during our regular season to pay what they can."

Maria's eyes widened, "Wouldn't you lose money."

"Lots of it, I'm afraid."

"I am not surprised the board is against it."

"They want the income difference to come out of my salary," Henry admitted. "And I don't make as much as people think."

"But you are the star!"

"I am only one of many stars in the orchestra and also our vocal musicians. Being a singer, I am sure you've heard of Katie or Beth?" Henry questioned. "They are also considered some of the best vocalists in the world."

"Yes, I can only wish to be as good," Maria admitted. "I have been to a few concerts where they were performing and I have to admit, I'm a bit jealous. Although, I do believe I can sing very well."

"I'd love to hear you sing sometime," Henry smiled. "Our chorus is open for auditions."

"That is very kind of you to offer, and I may take you up on that. Although, my focus is singing for my church."

"Praising the Lord with your voice," Henry understood. "Well, there isn't a far more important job than that."

"Agreed," Maria glanced down at their clasping hands.

"You are so beautiful, Maria." Henry said, then he suddenly burst into singing very softly, "Yes, so 'how do we solve a problem like Maria'…"

"I am a problem?" Maria asked.

"In so many ways," Henry said.

"In what ways?"

Suddenly, he leaned over and kissed her lips. She could

barely believe it. She backed away in shock.

"I am sorry." Henry said.

It took a moment for her to come to her senses. She touched her lips. "You kissed me?"

"I am your employer, and I shouldn't have. I am sorry with all this going on with Pulse and your brother, I guess I am just a little bit out of my senses."

"Don't be sorry," Maria said, then she giggled. "That was quite wonderful."

"It was?"

Suddenly two waiters appeared and began to serve them their plates with no silverware they were to eat with their fingers. Maria touched her chicken, but it was too hot to touch. She looked for a napkin and realized there wasn't one.

"This will be messy," Henry laughed.

"Yes, I do believe so."

"Sometimes a bit messy is good," he said.

Maria wondered if he was still referring to the food or the fact that something between them was growing. It was something Maria had never felt before and it was pulling her directly into his world.

CHAPTER 18

With a curious look on his face, police detective Arnie Williams, sat across the table. He was an average size man, with dark hair, fair skin with light blue eyes. I was surprised by the phone call this afternoon that I was to meet him this evening at the Golden Swan restaurant to talk further about the missing Stradivarius. As the detective took out his notebook, he gave me an explanation as to why he wanted to converse with me alone.

"I've been assigned to the case of the missing violin, Mrs. Coggins, so I'd like to know the backgrounds of all the people involved. History then points out some facts that lead me to a new direction in the investigation."

I gulped, nervous about his first question. "You do realize that it isn't just any violin. It is a Stradivarius owned by PSO's Kazuo Hiroki, one of the finest violinists in the world, and my husband's reputation as a conductor of the PSO is on the line."

"Yes, the instrument is worth four and a half million dollars," Detective Williams looked me in the eye. "Your husband was aware of that fact. So, how did you and your husband Henry meet? You've only been married a few months now. Isn't that correct?"

My mind drifted back to our first meeting. He came into my life like a song, a melody so ultimately beautiful that Beethoven himself couldn't have created such a masterpiece. His name was Doctor Henry Coggins, and he was the very talented and famous Director of the Palms Symphony

Orchestra on the Space Coast of Florida. That's what I wanted to tell him --I had never been happier in my life --until the violin was stolen.

Detective Williams interjected, "My wife is a season ticket holder and I read your wedding announcement in the newspaper."

"How wonderful that you are a supporter of the PSO. The Rouse concert is scheduled for this Saturday, you know."

"Her husband is so talented," the waiter commented, leaning over the white-clothed table as he waited for our order.

"There'll be many officers in attendance, including me, for this one," informed Detective Williams, waving the waiter away. "You were about to tell me of your first meeting, Mrs. Coggins."

"We met only three months ago at a marketing meeting."

I recalled that moment like yesterday when I fell in love with him. "He just glanced over at me. He stopped speaking mid-sentence. Our eyes met, and I just knew. This man would be important to me for the rest of my life. We stared at each other for a moment."

"So, it was love at first sight," Detective Williams wrote in his notebook. "Is that when he asked you out?"

I lightly chuckled, "It happened so fast. He was so good to my family when my brother was endangered at Pulse. I fell in love seeing how kind and caring he was."

"Interesting," the detective said. "You two also have a love of music in common."

"Music is essential to us."

"That is a beautiful love story," Detective Williams commented softly. "Almost sounds too good to be true," Detective Williams glanced up for a moment, then jotted another line on his notepad.

CHAPTER 19

Interrupting my pleasant memory, a second waiter approached carrying a wireless phone. "Mrs. Maria Coggins? I hope this call gives news of the missing violin. The theft is headlining the *Florida Times* newspaper this morning."

"Call me Maria," I placed the receiver to my ear while pointing to Detective Williams. "The police are starting the official investigation tonight."

"Hello, Love," he whispered.

Recognizing my husband's voice on the phone, I replied from my chair in the Golden Swan restaurant, "Are you okay? I've been waiting an hour."

"I can't make it for dinner, Love."

"You're not coming," I asked disappointedly.

"The flute concerto by Rouse needs more time and Hiroki's Sunshine Rail hasn't even arrived yet," my husband explained. "I am going to have to send a cab to pick him up because the police are questioning the orchestra section by section."

"When is Hiroki's rail coming in?" I asked, knowing I was near the station. "I'll pick up your violinist, pack some dinner for us, and we can eat right in the Beaumont auditorium on a rehearsal break."

"You're sexier than Mozart," he commented.

Knowing that was his divine flattery, I laughed. "Love

you, Maestro."

"Oh, by the way, Kazuo means Harmony in Japanese, but don't expect any peace from him with what's happening."

"I can handle it. See you soon. Bye." I returned the phone to the waiter. "Thank you. It appears that I will have to place my order to go." Focusing my attention back to the detective. "I'm sorry, Mr. Williams, but it appears that your department is questioning the PSO and causing a delay in my husband's rehearsal. He works very hard and deserves a dinner break. Perhaps we should join them."

"Oh, I had hoped to spend more time alone finding out your background," Detective Williams said. "But you are right; we will continue this evening. I have another person to question; then I will be headed to the Beaumont Auditorium to continue the orchestra interview. One hundred people put in a lot of effort. I'm glad your husband understands and the PSO is cooperating."

The second waiter retreated, and then the first one reappeared with his pen and pad. "What can I get you to go, Mrs. Coggins?"

"I'd like two chicken cordon blue specials with rosemary potatoes and asparagus. Anything for you, Mr. Williams?"

"How sweet of you. It's been quite a long time since someone as beautiful as you, Maria, offered to buy my dinner. But no, thank you."

Completely flattered, I had just stuffed myself into a fuchsia dress, hoping that it would hide the fact my tan was fading, and had hardly even brushed my long black curly hair.

"I'm sorry to hear about the PSO's missing violin." The waiter who had brought me the phone jotted down my request, and his brown eyes suddenly filled with tears. "Did your husband ever tell you that he stopped someone from hurting himself by jumping off the bridge?"

"Now that's quite a background story," the detective interjected. "Gives me some depth into the director's character."

"You don't have to worry about Henry Coggin's character. He is a great man. He's kind to everyone regardless of race, age, disability, or sexual preference." The waiter explained. "Your husband stopped his Porsche, and instead of screaming 'jump,' like all those other idiots at the bottom of the bridge, he yelled something quite peculiar."

"What did he yell?" I asked.

"Don't pull a Tchaikovsky," the waiter replied.

"What does that even mean?" Detective Williams wondered aloud.

The waiter continued," I was a cellist for the PSO their first year, and we performed the Tchaikovsky Symphony No. 6. During rehearsal, Director Henry explained to us that Tchaikovsky killed himself because it was about to come out that he was a gay man. Tchaikovsky had just written the Symphony No. 6 before he committed suicide. Now, six is recognized to this day as Tchaikovsky's best composition. At rehearsal, your husband kept saying, 'Imagine if Tchaikovsky hadn't killed himself and written more beautiful masterpieces! His death should be a lesson that no matter how horrible life can be, remember to hang on and wait for the next composition.'"

Tears suddenly stung my eyes. "So, you were the cellist on the bridge about to jump?"

"His words 'Don't pull a Tchaikovsky' meant that there may be more symphonies for me and not to end it now. Tchaikovsky never knew that everyone would come to love his No. 6 best. He never lived long enough to know he would be revered forever."

"I'm glad the Maestro helped you," the Detective concluded.

"I'm playing Beethoven No. 5 in C minor with the PSO. Director Coggins is a great man, and he would have never stolen that violin from Hiroki!"

I smiled. "I'll see you again."

"Please do it at the spring concert," he said. "I'll check on your dinner."

The waiter walked away. I watched the stranger for several minutes, wondering if my husband had not driven by that bridge, would this man still be here today?

"The words your husband had said to him were genius and something this man would understand, 'Don't pull a Tchaikovsky.' Brilliant." Detective Williams concluded. "I'll see you later, Mrs. Coggins," he rose from the table and walked away with a slight limp on the right side as if his knee had been injured.

A few minutes later, my dinner arrived in a white bag. I thanked the waiter but before I left, he reached out and gave me an unexpected hug. "I'll see you for Beethoven then."

"If not before. Thank you for standing up for my husband."

"Anything for the Maestro," he winked.

Across the street, I walked to the black Porsche and stuffed the bag into the tiny trunk. I wished I had taken the Ferrari instead now that I knew I'd pick up a guest from the station. Glancing at my watch, which read 7:00 PM, I got behind the wheel and hurried downtown until I arrived at the Sunshine Rail Florida train station.

Standing outside was the older Asian gentleman whom I had recognized from the first night I had met my husband but whom I hadn't seen since our wedding. A shorter man with big, black-rimmed glasses, he maintained a small pot belly which he stuffed into a tailored three-piece suit. In his hand, he carried his replacement violin in a black patent case instead of the ancient beige one that once contained the Stradivarius.

"Hello, Mr. Hiroki," opening my car door, I said. "It appears that I am your ride tonight. The police are investigating the disappearance of your violin as we speak. The orchestra is being detained and questioned."

"As well they should be," he spoke in perfect English, then hurried around to the side of my car. He plopped in and placed the violin case between his legs, leaving him no room. "So much is expected of me during this disaster. It is the least the PSO can do."

"Would you like me to place your violin in the trunk?"

He gave me what could only be described as an angry stink face. "If it were my Stradivarius then no, but I suppose this one would be fine in a trunk."

Knowing his missing violin was considered one of the

most valuable violins in the world and he had the right to be devastated, "I'm so sorry. The police will find your beloved instrument, I'm sure."

"The Stradivarius was given in 1812 to my great, great, great grandfather as a gift. It has belonged to my family for generations."

"I am quite aware."

"To me, it is priceless," He looked up from behind his big-rimmed black glasses. "Heirloom Society of New York valued it as worth nearly five million dollars. I realize you are the PSO Conductor's wife, but please shall we…I am late for the Rouse rehearsal and want to speak to the detective in charge of the investigation, Detective Williams."

CHAPTER 20

When we arrived at the Beaumont Auditorium in Palm Bay, the Marquee scrolled in big, bold gold letters, **PALMS SYMPHONY ORCHESTRA, VIVALDI & ROUSE, FRIDAY & SATURDAY-SOLD OUT.**

The auditorium doors were closed, but I recognized Katherine Croff standing in front of the building. Her long dark blonde hair flowed straight to her waist, and she was wearing a long red tight-fitting dress that mimicked a 30s flapper style. "Katie felt good enough to make it," I commented.

"That is fantastic news," Mr. Hiroki exclaimed. "I heard you spent several hours with her at the hospital last night. I was surprised because I had heard rumors that a few orchestra chorus singers don't like Katie Croff."

Denying that I did have a little jealousy, I added, "That is ridiculous. There are no problems between the chorus singers and Katie." Ms. Croft had been the one chosen by the PSO board to sing our National Anthem throughout the season. Of course, she has a perfect figure and can sing like a nightingale, too. A month ago, I even questioned if Henry might have once dated Katie before me. I wasn't surprised there were rumors.

"Katie looks as good as new," Mr. Hiroki said.

I parked the Porsche in the spot marked RESERVED FOR MAESTRO COGGINS, and Katie rushed over. She bent over practically falling out of her low-cut dress; Mr. Hiroki clearly didn't mind getting attention.

He said, "Hello, Katherine. I'm so glad you are all right."

"Good evening, Mr. Hiroki. I'm so sorry about your beautiful violin."

"Such a dear, sweet girl," he smiled, his eyes glancing down. He got out of the vehicle, grabbed the violin out of the trunk, and offered his arm for her to take.

Accepting the offered violin case, she asked, "Are you sure I should continue, Mr. Hiroki? If you don't trust me anymore, I would understand."

"Of course, I trust you." Mr. Hiroki hugged her.

Even though I had liked Katie, I sighed softly. Yes, envious I was of Katie's incredible beauty and talent. She had become a good friend who even offered to sing at my wedding. Usually, she charges a significant amount for an appearance.

I exited the Porsche and grabbed my big white dinner bag. Entering the Beaumont auditorium, I heard the orchestra playing Vivaldi's *Spring* from the first movement of the *Four Seasons*. My husband wore a dark shirt and black denim jeans, waving his baton in front of the orchestra.

For a moment, I stopped to watch how breathtakingly handsome a man he was, tall, with brown hair, and so masculine. The passionate expressions on his face were truly magical to watch. Every movement of his hands and eyes showed his love for every brilliantly written note.

After the piece finished, Henry Coggins smiled. "All right, that is our encore song if they give us a standing O." He saw me approaching from the corner of his eye. "Let's take a fifteen-minute break. We'll finish by repeating the Rouse flute concerto, then call it a night."

The string section began to disperse as well as the two double bass players. Henry strode over and gently kissed my lips. "Hello, Love."

"Can I steal you away?" I asked.

"You have my full attention for at least fifteen minutes," Henry said.

I glanced at Mr. Hiroki, opening his violin case with Katie to his right. "She seems to be getting back into the swing of things."

"Katie?" Henry chuckled. "Still worrying about her? Wouldn't you think it better for a bit of piano time later?"

His sexual innuendo made me giggle and blush. "Last time was delightful."

"Did you see the marquee outside? We are completely sold out!" my husband announced. "I had to turn away about a dozen college students. I'm going to remind the board again that we need to increase performance nights and give music students free access. Everyone should be able to hear symphony music, not just those who can afford the hundred-dollar tickets."

"You've mentioned the free student idea before to the board," I reminded.

"I want to share symphony music and teach our next generation that classical music can be as fun as rock-in-roll."

"Fun?" I smiled. "I just drove fifteen minutes with Mr. Hiroki and he is devastated about his Stradivarius. That was not fun."

A tall woman in a brown suit approached us and opened my husband's dressing room door. "Excuse me. Sorry to interrupt, but I have a question for you, Mrs. Coggins. My name is Officer Lenore Peterson. I'm working on Arnie Williams' team."

Together, we stepped into a dressing room. I began setting our dinner boxes in front of the lighted mirror, wishing I had more alone time with my husband.

Henry sat down on one of the four stools and asked. "Mr. Williams has already interviewed my wife earlier. Must she be questioned more tonight?"

"I'm sorry but I must ask her what I asked of each orchestra member. What exactly did you see last night, Mrs. Coggins? When did you first notice something wasn't right?"

I sighed, "I was sitting in the auditorium in the third row, waiting for Henry and the PSO to finish the rehearsal. Then I heard a loud scream that I knew it could have come only from Katie. I looked over and saw her on the floor, next to the big red curtain."

"What did you do?"

"I screamed, 'I think Katie's fainted. Call 9-1-1! I rushed down the aisle up the stairs. By the time I arrived, Henry was already kneeling, checking for a pulse on her neck."

"Katie had one," stated Detective Peterson.

"Yes, but she looked very pale," Henry said. "Then I saw the syringe in her side, sticking out like a dart."

"Let me ask you again, Mrs. Coggins. How did you feel about Katherine Croff? Were you glad?" Detective Peterson asked.

"Of course not!" I gasped.

"The police were told that a few of the ladies who might have tried out to sing for the PSO could be jealous that Katie was the one chosen soloist for the national anthem," Detective Peterson commented.

"How dare you!" I roared.

"My wife is very talented," Henry interrupted. "This is way out of line. Marie had nothing to do with the stolen violin or Katie's attack."

"I spent half the night with her in the hospital," I protested. "Katie is my friend."

"My wife would never hurt anyone, and I was the one who called for help," he added.

"Yes, I heard the 9-1-1 recording. 'A PSO singer has been attacked. Please send an ambulance to Beaumont right away,'" Detective Peterson repeated the words he had spoken.

"Katie is in her early thirties and as far as I know, she has no history of any serious diseases. The hospital is running a blood analysis, but it appears a knock-out drug might have been used to snatch the violin out of Katie's hands," alerted Detective Peterson. "Does Katie always follow Mr. Hiroki around like that?"

Henry informed, "Katie is very well-loved by Hiroki. He trusts her to watch his instruments. She has even been specially trained to handle his Stradivarius locking case security system. That's why I noticed right away that the violin was missing. Hiroki had just stepped out to use the restroom, and Katie was clutching an empty case."

"So, carrying his violin case is normal for her to do?" Detective Peterson asked.

"Yes, Katie and Mr. Hiroki have been friends for many years. Whoever stole the violin knew Katie would be the one guarding this week," Henry acknowledged. "They didn't care if she got hurt in the process."

Detective Peterson suddenly glanced over at me. "How many solos have you been scheduled to perform this PSO season, Mrs. Coggins?"

My eyes tightened on the detective's face, trying to hide my rage at her line of questioning, "None."

CHAPTER 21

"My wife is singing, *O Rest in the Lord*, by Mendelssohn this fall," Henry announced to detective Peterson.

"*O Rest in the Lord* is an alto solo? Who is singing '*O Hear Ye Israel*'?"

He cleared his throat, "Betty Redvine."

"Oh, again, your wife gets passed up for a leading soprano solo," the detective commented.

"I had to audition in front of the board. My husband isn't the only deciding factor here."

"If it were up to me, I would have given her every solo," he smiled. "There are many very talented vocalists in Florida, Detective. Fontina Walker, Chelsey Lean, Barb Knots, Lee Dodson, Betty Redvine, Mark Baer, Dotty Wrights, Nancy Brocks, Brittany Perdew to name a few. The PSO tries our best to give our audience the best performers, along with college music majors, a chance to shine. I assure you there isn't a problem."

My eyes fell to the floor and the detective noticed my sudden uncomfortableness. In professional music, competition is par for the course, whether for a chair in the orchestra or a vocal solo. Hurt feelings because you didn't get the chair or song you wanted are never acknowledged publicly. Emotions are kept below the surface because it's understood good sportsmanship and those who have God-given talent and work hard should share the spotlight.

"Katie Croff has her music series at the playhouse. You

aren't even a little upset?"

Not wanting to answer, I repeated. "I am Katie's friend. I rode with her to the hospital and was very concerned about her health."

"Why did you go with Katie in the ambulance? The EMT wasn't even sure you were friends, Mrs. Coggins."

A sudden memory of the EMT made me snap. "Seriously! The EMT would not stop staring at Katie's breasts and he didn't even look up to ask what happened. He kept his hand on her neck, checking her pulse, and his eyes stayed two inches from her cleavage. Not very professional. Of course, I was very concerned about the needle stuck in Katie's side. The EMT stayed focused on her giant breasts. I finally decided to ask him. 'Shouldn't you remove that?'"

"They'll remove her bra when she gets to the hospital," he said.

"Not the bra, the needle stuck in her side!" I yelled at him. "His hands fumbled around Katie's stomach and examined what had been stuck in her side. Then he placed the needle in a Ziploc bag and said, 'Melbourne CSI will be sure to test for what was inside the dart.'"

"What did you suspect might be in the syringe," the detective asked.

"The EMT told me that Katie's blood pressure was down but her pulse was still strong, so he thought that whatever it was just put her to sleep for a while, a sedative of some kind."

"The EMT mostly just questioned me. 'Is that her name, Katie? Is she married? Does she have a boyfriend?'"

Out cold and still getting more attention than me! I had thought to myself. "Last I heard, Katie was dating the bassoon player for the Palms Symphony Orchestra or was it the oboe player? Nope, that's right, it was half the cello section."

The detective laughed through her ebony lips. "If you don't care for her, why did you insist on going in the ambulance and consulting the EMT?"

I rolled my eyes. "I like Katherine…and she was supposed to sing tomorrow night."

"So, the concert is what you were worried about. She's singing the national anthem and you're not," the detective said.

I snipped. "I was concerned for my husband's concert and her health. That EMT even insulted me!"

"Did he now?" Detective Peterson asked. "You must not have liked that."

"He asked me. Do you know Henry Coggins, the Concertmaster of the PSO? I heard that he just got married to some bitch with an attitude problem."

"So, what did you do?" the detective inquired.

I asked him. "Do you even know who I am?"

"Nope," he replied. "Then he pushed some buttons on the monitor and rechecked Katie's pulse. He said, 'She might be out for longer than we expected. I don't like how she's breathing either.'"

"So what happened then?" the detective realized.

"I didn't ask him another question. I observed as he

continued to watch Katie's chest. Her breathing at times got shallow, and it wasn't very comforting when he suddenly pulled out an oxygen mask. I was glued to her every breath as well. I even prayed at some point. When we arrived at the hospital, Katie was immediately wheeled on the stretcher to a private ER room by the EMT. The EMT left, and several nurses rushed to exam Katie. Several times, a policeman checked in the doorway to ask if she was responsive yet."

"So you do care for her?"

"Katie hadn't moved an inch since she'd been drugged. I had hoped the drug would have left her system by now. Forgetting everything, I held her hand. Katie stirred a little, which gave me hope. I checked her face and saw a flutter of one long eyelash."

Then the doctor rushed in and quickly commented, "Wow, no one told me they brought Sleeping Beauty in here. Isn't this Katie Croft, the singer?"

Quickly, I informed him, "Katie hasn't said a word for several hours and does seem to be in somewhat distressed breathing. I would appreciate some professionalism, Sir!"

"I was supposed to see Katie singing at the PSO tomorrow night and…Oh, you are Mrs. Coggins, the wife of Henry Coggins, right? My name is Dr. Jefferson. My brother played trumpet and took some classes at the university."

I begged that doctor, "Can you please help my friend?"

"We took a blood sample, and it looks like she may have an animal toxin in her system. She may be groggy for a day or two, though. We'll give her some IVs and keep her for the rest of the night to ensure the drug leaves her kidneys safely."

"I see."

"You should be watching the news now." He grabbed the hospital's small television remote. "Your husband is talking to the media about the missing Stradivarius violin."

The small hospital television screen flashed, and I saw my husband talking to a reporter. The doctor turned up the volume for the newsman to ask him, "Director Coggins, does anyone in the PSO know who has taken the priceless heirloom?"

"At this time, all of us at the PSO are thinking of Katie Croff, who is struggling to regain consciousness. We are all hopeful that Katie saw who has stolen the violin so that the police can quickly return the instrument to Mr. Hiroki undamaged."

The newscast returned to the newsroom. Proudly, I smiled, thinking how handsome he appeared on television and that he had put on a purple tie just for the occasion. His deep voice spoke so clearly. My husband did seem very concerned about Katie and catching the thief. It was only then that I noticed his right-hand shaking. Henry was distraught.

CHAPTER 22

When she walked in carrying a bouquet of roses, I was surprised. I recognized her face and could picture her playing the harp, but I couldn't recall her name without a PSO program. She was a large woman, about six foot one; her hair cut short above the ears in a blonde bob.

"Hello, Maria," she greeted me. "How is Katie?"

"Not sure," I said.

"The police suspect that it must have been someone in the symphony who stole the violin and hurt Katie," she added.

"It couldn't have been a PSO member," I said, surprisingly.

"Since the rehearsal was closed tonight, that is what the police suspect," she repeated.

"My husband directs over one hundred people a year, and I have forgotten your name. I know you play the harp."

"Oh, I'm Marlene. I play in the PSO when asked. Normally, I work on weekends doing Music Therapy in the hospitals and nursing homes."

"I didn't know this hospital hired musicians."

"They do on the hospice wing. The harp is a very calming instrument that helps families deal with serious illnesses. My playing brings great comfort. I get requests for a lot of Celtic music and hymns."

"That's wonderful," I smiled. "Are those flowers for Katie? Those roses are so beautiful."

"No, your husband heard I was on my way here and gave them to me to give you. He told me to remind you that the piano needs cleaning."

I blushed, thankful she didn't know what that meant. "I see."

"Must be a pretty messy piano for him to be that concerned," Marlene added. "Is your white Bosendorfer Grand going to be used during the Rouse and Vivaldi?"

"Not this concert," my arms embraced the beautiful roses of every color, a rainbow of roses; I'd never seen such unique flowers before. "Thank you for bringing them. They are quite spectacular!"

"You're very blessed to have the Maestro," Marlene said. "It's wonderful to see a couple who loves each other and are also good friends."

"Yes," I admitted, "we are friends, and I do love him."

"Did you know there have been studies showing that harp music improves brain stimulation?" Marlene grinned. "I should get my smaller harp out of my car and play some songs for Katie!"

"Yes, it is worth a try," I agreed, watching her leave.

Suddenly, a moan escaped Katie's lips. I rushed over to her bedside and leaned over. "Katie, can you hear me?"

I waited and waited to no avail.

After a few minutes, Marlene returned. She plopped into a metal chair and unwrapped a small hand-held harp from a soft leather case. Slowly, she began to strum. I listened carefully and then recognized the tune *Moon River* by Henry Mancini. "Oh, I love this song!"

"It's one of the favorites; I often have that song requested when I play harp in the nursing homes."

"Moon…River…" I suddenly burst out into song, "Wider than a smile. I'm crossing you in style someday."

"Oh, God help me," came from the lips of a woman thought to have nearly comatose. Katie's eyes fluttered open wide. "Please don't tell me I am in heaven and that's what angels sound like these days."

I laughed. "Katie! You know it's me."

Katie suddenly smiled. "Then you know I'm joking."

"Yes."

"Only a great diva like you can take it," Katie sat up straight. "I feel like I have slept for days. Why am I even here? Is this the hospital?"

"You collapsed," Marlene announced.

"I did?"

"You passed out right after someone nailed you with a drug-filled needle and stole Mr. Hiroki's Stradivarius."

The pure look of horror crossed Katherine Croff's terrified face. Katie didn't know the violin had been stolen, which meant one thing: Katie didn't know the plan to steal the violin. If her testimony was the only thing that could assist the police in finding Mr. Hiroki's precious instrument, the PSO is in big trouble.

"Am I going to be, okay?" Katie gasped, suddenly feeling her stomach. "Oh, my side hurts."

"You'll be fine."

"Are those for me?" Katie asked, gazing at the roses in my arms.

I handed them to her. "They are from Henry and me. Please rest up; you've got a performance tomorrow night at Rouse & Vivaldi."

She shook her head. "What if this criminal comes after me again? I'm not going out publicly until the culprit is behind bars!"

I should have been crushed. I know, but a sudden thrill ran down my spine. If Katherine Croff decided not to sing at the PSO concert, that could leave an opening for a singer to do the national anthem. *Could I be the one to sing for the PSO when they are expecting thousands of people?* Suddenly, I felt awful seeing her in the hospital bed.

"You'd better tell Director Coggins that you might not be able to sing then," Marlene said, interrupting my selfish thoughts.

"Don't worry," I wrapped an arm around Katie's shoulders. "You just rest. The police will find that criminal. I'm sure."

"And what if they don't?" Katie gasped. "I won't want to leave this hospital room!"

Two days later, Detective Lenore Peterson slowly placed a pencil behind her left black ear at Coggin's seaside home, listening to my explanation of what happened after the Stradivarius was stolen and at the hospital. "Yet, Katie returned tonight."

"She's not singing tomorrow," my husband suddenly announced in the dressing room. "Katie only came to rehearsal tonight since the police were going to be here and talk to Mr. Hiroki. She wanted him to know she had nothing to do with the crime. Plus, Katie doesn't believe anyone in the PSO would harm her, and neither do I."

"Who will be her replacement?" I asked.

The detective asked, "Let me guess who wants to be."

"Betty Redvine will be," my husband announced. "She is under contract to be Katie's understudy this season. Katie will return to singing the national anthem at the next concert. Hopefully, by then, this nightmare will be over, and the violin will have been returned."

The detective glanced over, and I knew not to show any disappointment. The fact the detective suspected me due to some perceived vengefulness was utterly wrong. Many singers at all different talent levels might have been considered and I didn't have any desire to hurt anyone, especially someone I did feel a friend.

"Director Coggins, we need you to remain after rehearsal tonight so that we can inform you about a few PSO members' criminal backgrounds."

Henry shook his head, "Can't this wait until after the Rouse & Vivaldi concert series."

"No, I'm afraid not."

"I'll take a cab and leave the car for you, Love," I said, watching the detective rise from her stool and leave the dressing room.

"This is going to be a long night," he murmured, "a very, very long night."

As my husband began to dine on his dinner, I wondered which performers in the orchestra had a criminal past. Criminal background checks weren't a requirement to be an instrumentalist or a singer for the PSO. Their lack of this procedure was clearly to my benefit.

CHAPTER 23

While I was standing on the curb outside the Beamount Auditorium a few minutes later, a yellow cab drove up and I immediately recognized the driver. It was none other than Larry Hillman.

Larry Hillman and I dated in high school. We met in Intermediate Algebra class and since I was so awful at Mathematics, he offered to tutor me. After a few sessions, we kissed and became high school sweethearts. A year later, Larry was recruited to play college football and then he started tutoring another girl who was horrible at algebra. Although my feelings have changed for him since I married Henry, I still enjoy running into him occasionally.

Quickly, Larry jumped out of the driver's seat. Bald and with a short brown goatee, he'd kept all his muscles from playing high school and college football.

"Hi, Maria," he opened the passenger side door on the left side of the car. "Where's Beethoven?"

"My husband, the Director of the PSO, does not need a ride tonight, and besides the real Beethoven was deaf and wrote entire symphonies," I said, opening the front door to sit directly beside him.

"You're not supposed to stay in front." He came around the car to sit behind the wheel. "But I won't tell the boss if you won't."

He started the engine, and I noticed that the gold ring he used to wear on his left hand was no longer there. I had heard that he had gotten a divorce and that his wife had taken his house but not his fishing boat.

"It's good to see you, Larry."

"So, Rouse and Vivaldi, huh," he said. "I'm a rock-in-roll, heavy metal guy myself, remember?"

I recalled the night we slept outside the ticket store to get Motley Crue tickets. That evening, he promised to love me forever while we listened to "Home Sweet Home." Interrupting my flooding memories, I said, "Since returning for college classes as a Music Major, I have learned all kinds of interesting facts about classical music. Beethoven was so deaf that he put his ear to the piano to hear the vibrations so he could compose."

"If the song doesn't have an electric guitar, I don't need to hear it."

I glanced over to Larry and noticed his brilliant smile. There was still something twinkling in his golden-brown eyes. It was hard for me to turn my attention back to the road. When the butterflies churned in my stomach, I realized I was still attracted to him after all these years.

"I don't know about you singing all that classical stuff, but I remember the night I kissed you at that beach club. Wow, you could dance back then and sing rock, too. You sure had the pipes."

"Larry, I'm married now. We shouldn't talk about the past."

"In my opinion, we are our past. You can't deny that we were once a cool couple. Everyone in town knows I was the fool who left the best thing that ever happened to me."

I smiled.

"Don't worry, I know Mr. Beethoven is your new man. I've just had it pretty rough lately. Sorry to reminisce."

"Don't apologize. I never regretted the time we had together." I admitted. "We had fun. Somehow, you made it easier to learn all those linear equations."

He reached out and nearly held my hand.

Shocked by his forwardness, I suddenly felt very uncomfortable and pulled my hand back toward my body. Luckily, I noticed we were turning the corner not far from my home.

"If they don't find that violin and the PSO is found responsible, your new husband will lose just about everything he has to pay back Mr. Hiroki. Will you stay if he doesn't have all that money and fame?"

I gasped. "How dare you! I love Henry."

"Coggin's a playboy," he reminded me.

"Henry is no such thing."

"Haven't you heard those stories about him dating models from Miami and all those parties?"

"Those are just rumors!" I gasped.

"Why do you think he picked you out of all the hot broads in this town?"

"Because I'm a wonderful person," I countered, "with a

big heart."

He was going to say something. I could tell that something was right on his tongue's tip. Instead, he gave me a look like I was not going to continue this conversation and leaned back into the driver's seat, taking a deep breath. "I'm sorry. You know, your life is…your life with Beethoven."

"By the way, I love the real Beethoven, too. The PSO will be fabulous performing the No. 5 in C Minor this spring. When you're done listening to AC/DC, you might want to come out and give another type of music a chance. You might start to like the symphony! Everyone in the PSO has mastered their instrument to sound amazing. All those talented musicians need incredible skill to unite and make that magic happen. It's like a miracle!"

Larry pulled the cab into the driveway of my two-story house at the end of Maple Drive, which overlooked the Indian River Lagoon.

"Back at your mansion," he said, "miracle lady."

"You are still bitter over our breakup, aren't you?" I tried to hide my disappointment. "Just remember, you were the one who left me, not the other way around. You left me."

He didn't bother exiting the cab to open my door. I waited a moment. When he didn't move, I opened the car door myself and rose just in time to hear him tag, "I never really left."

CHAPTER 24

Jennifer opened the door of the Palms Symphony Orchestra office. The night sky shined brightly with a full moon and twinkling stars as far as the eye could see over the Indian River Lagoon. She looked like a mess. Her short gray hair was frazzled and uncombed. She wore a loose sundress with sneakers, and her everyday makeup didn't seem perfect. There were large bags under her eyes.

"You, okay?"

"Yeah," Jennifer, the music Librarian said. "I am sorry it took so long to answer the door. I thought I heard something but didn't want to look in the library alone. Thank goodness you all have come."

Heather smiled and pointed to a young teenager with long, straight brown hair wearing jeans with a black T-shirt that introduced, "This is Bradly. He'll be working the voice recorder."

"Come on in," Jennifer said, noticing her multi-colored hair. Today, it was purple and pink.

"On such short notice, I couldn't get Gary to come. He's our paranormal group's founder. He said he might be able to come next weekend and will bring more equipment. He even has a heat device."

"My specialty is EVPs." Bradly said. "You have already heard voices."

"Yes," Jennifer said, moving inside to stand next to the music library door. "I need you to get proof so I can show

Henry."

"They are having a hard time believing you."

"They are," Jennifer admitted. "Most people think I'm crazy about this and it is just a way to keep others away from the safe."

Heather couldn't help but notice how desperate she was sounding, "Are you sure you are ready to deal with this tonight? With all that's going on with…"

"The phone's been ringing off the hook with people claiming they might know who took Hiroki's violin or asking if Katie is okay," Jennifer admitted. "But I need to document this to prove to Henry we need to get a priest in here."

"The ghost needs to accept his or her death and move into the light," Brad stated.

"I must admit, after seeing the writing on the ceiling, that I am becoming afraid of being here, especially alone or at night. I have a job to do!"

Heather nodded her multi-colored head with understanding, "Having paranormal activity can be distracting."

"It can drive you nuts trying to figure things out or what the ghost wants, so let's tackle this head-on and try to solve your problem." Bradly said, "Have you ever been scratched, pulled or pushed?"

"Nothing harmful," Jennifer said. "I feel it is a late musician because it seems to know about the music and even makes suggestions on what our musicians should play. It seems to communicate in ways I understand."

"Really?" Bradly scratched his head. "It could be a ghost who knows you then."

Heather gasped, "That's true! It may be attached to you. Has anything happened at a different location like your house?"

"No," Jennifer said. "Oh, please, do you think it could follow me home."

"Does it just stay in the library?" Bradly pulled out a large recorder and placed headphones over one ear.

"I've only noticed weird things happening in the library," Jennifer unlocked the door. "Will that record proof?'

"Yes," Bradly stated. "I'll be able to download the track and enhance it. This recording device will capture any sound, even if it is weak. Don't worry. We'll get you proof so you can convince your boss to call in a priest or a medium."

"Thank goodness," Jennifer said. "Well, here is the library. Feel free to do whatever you need. Just don't move the painting where the safe is."

Bradly walked in, "Oh, you can feel the energy."

"I felt that too," Heather said.

"It's like being in a thunderstorm waiting for the next lightning strike," Jennifer said. "It's gotten stronger and usually I get goose bumps and sometimes it gets…"

Suddenly, everyone could see Jennifer's breath in the room.

Heather finished her sentence, "Cold."

"You've got a ghost," Bradly announced.

"Can you hear something?" Heather stated.

"I better start the recording," Bradly said.

"What do you hear?" Jennifer asked.

"I hear moaning," Bradly said.

"Does it sound male or female?" Heather watched as he placed the other earmuff over his ear.

"Male. It's male and sounds old." Brad said, then suddenly he started laughing. "Sorry, didn't mean to insult you."

"What is going on?" Jennifer gasped.

"The ghost told me that he's older than dirt." Brad stated, "I got that on tape, so we have proof already."

"Ask him why he is here and who is he?" Jennifer gasped. "Tell him to leave me alone and stop haunting the symphony library!"

Bradly's eyes widened. "He said something about Mozart; then he mumbled a few words. I can enhance that back in my studio. Maybe we can figure that out." He walked toward the bust of Mozart on the last filing cabinet.

"Night musket?" Bradly seemed to question what he was hearing.

"Serenade No. 13, Eine Kleine Nacht-Music," Jennifer sighed. "It's one of Mozart's most famous pieces of music. Is that why he haunts us? Because he loves classical music."

"It just said your name," Bradly gasped. "He's saying,

Jennifer. I am here."

"Who? What do you want?" Jennifer cried out in desperation. "Why do you keep bothering me?"

Bradly suddenly removed his headphones, and his eyes tightened on Jennifer.

"What?" Heather grabbed him.

"He just said, Uncle. Is this your uncle?"

Jennifer nearly fainted and grabbed a filing cabinet to keep herself on her feet. "It can't be. My Uncle Max was a Music Teacher and died a year ago of a massive heart attack."

"So, he died suddenly?" Heather asked.

"Yes, and he wasn't a very nice man…" Jennifer started to cry. Heather wrapped her arms around her, and Bradly put back on the headphones and asked a few more questions to what now seemed to be a ghost related to Jennifer.

CHAPTER 25

I spent the next few hours on the sofa in the Florida room watching television. Very upset, I barely glanced at the screen. There were too many questions that are unanswered. Why did Larry Hillman still have so much power over my senses? Who would do this to the PSO? Why was Katie attacked? Was it someone he knew?

Glancing at the moon shining through the giant glass window out onto a night-blackened sea, I heard the front door creak open. Across the room, I saw that the Lenox clock on the stand read midnight. Before I rose, Lenore Peterson and my husband were heading toward me.

"Good evening, Mrs. Coggins," the detective greeted. "We're sorry to have kept your husband so long tonight. We showed him the security video tape of the rehearsal at the Beaumont the night of the theft. Your husband confirmed all the PSO members in the video but I'd like you to take a look and see if there's someone he might have missed."

I let out a slow breath, glancing at the tall attractive African-American woman. "Of course, Detective."

My husband grabbed the DVD from the detective and set it into the DVD player underneath the flat-screen television.

Detective Peterson sat down on the sofa and motioned for me to do the same as she started the recording. "Look now; your husband just announced to take a short rehearsal break. You can see on the video that most of the musicians started getting up. But three went behind the velvet curtain. One oboe player, a trombonist, and the timpani player are now heading out of view. Katie Croff comes in at the right corner. See, she was walking beside Mr. Hiroki. He steps in front of her. A few seconds passed; he turns. Katie takes the violin case from him and hurries behind the curtain. Then, a loud scream can be heard. Katie's arm appears on the ground underneath the curtain, then her body and the empty violin case show. See there?"

"Oh, that's horrible," I exclaimed.

"Would you agree that only three people were near Ms. Croff and the violin backstage?" The Detective asked. "Director Coggins has identified them as Charlie McDaniel, Timpani player; Karl Canon, trombonist; and the oboe player, Mary Lot."

I gasped, "Mary Lot is a PEO society friend of mine. She goes to my church. She isn't capable of hurting anyone."

"I've known Karl since we went to Harvard together," Henry exclaimed. "He's got plenty of money from real estate. I honestly can't see Mary or Karl involved in this."

"So that leaves Charlie McDaniel," the Detective said. "Can you vouch for his character?"

My husband sat beside me and placed his arm around my shoulders. Feeling his touch calmed my pounding heart and made me feel at ease. "I don't know him personally."

"Charlie has been with the PSO since the beginning. He's even a member of the PSO and the county Music Education board," my husband announced.

"So, you believe that none of the three are capable of this violent act?" Detective Peterson asked.

"No, none of them," my husband concluded.

The detective stood. "Then I need a list of the backstage crew who worked that rehearsal and who will be backstage during tomorrow's concert?"

"I keep the employee forms at the PSO Office. They contain addresses, lists of phone numbers, and emails of all the PSO members and backstage sound crew at the Beaumont."

The Detective requisitioned. She paused the DVD directly on Charles McDaniel's perfectly featured freckled face. He was a giant man with bright red hair and a matching goatee. "I am unsure if you know this, but Charlie McDaniel has the worst of the PSO's criminal background."

"Yes, I know about his past two drug arrests. He studied music at Yale and jokes about his partying days. He's been drug-free for over twenty years now." My husband commented, "I can't complain about Charlie other than he thinks Yale has a better crew team than Harvard. He also is a real fan of the Spizzwinks."

"Oh, the Spizzwinks," Detective Peterson smiled. "The all-male singing group from Yale. Handsome fellows."

I knew Henry preferred Harvard, and anything that comes from Yale he detests as a thorn in his side. "My husband is not much for Yale. He is a Harvard man."

"Just a lot of college competitions in crew, I assure you. Can we get back to the questioning?" my husband asked.

"Touchy about Yale, I see. Let's watch another tape from the outside parking lot security camera." Detective Peterson placed another DVD in the machine and waited. "Here it is, Mrs. Coggins. The place is around the corner. During the attack, only one car moved in the parking lot; a yellow cab drove in from around the street corner."

"Cab?" I said, remembering Larry.

Suddenly, the detective went to the front door. Henry and I stood as she slowly opened it, and in walked Larry Hillman, followed by Detective Arnie Williams.

"Larry?" I gasped.

My husband questioned. "Isn't that your high school ex-boyfriend?"

"Chill, Beethoven, your wife didn't even know I would be the one driving her home from your rehearsal the other night," Larry stepped into the living room and stood before Henry.

I shook my head and asked. "Did someone call for a cab the night the violin was stolen? Why were you in the video then?"

"We could check with your employer to see if anyone requested a cab," Detective Peterson said to Larry.

Larry slightly shrugged and admitted. "There were no calls for a cab to the Beaumont the other night."

Detective Davis slapped my ex-boyfriend Larry on the back. "So why were you driving outside the Beaumont Auditorium the night the Stradivarius was stolen? Your cab's number is caught on tape, 0-6."

"I was there the night of the theft," Larry admitted.

It was all I could do to hide my shock.

CHAPTER 26

Detective Arnie Williams immediately commanded, "I think you need to come to the station for some further questioning, Larry."

"I didn't steal the violin. You can see on the tape --I didn't even get out of the cab."

"So why were you there?" I interrupted.

"My business," he said, frankly.

"Actually," Lenore Peterson smiled, "It's police business now and you need to come with me for further questioning."

Detective Williams grabbed his arm and led Larry Hillman to the door, followed closely by Detective Lenore Peterson. "Have a great night, Mr. & Mrs. Coggins. I'll be by the PSO office sometime tomorrow for the list of backstage employees," she tagged.

"That will be fine, Detective. Have a good evening." Henry nearly slammed the door shut after them.

The moment the house was clear of guests, my handsome husband moved to the parlor, sat down in front of our shiny Bosendorfer Imperial Grand piano made in 1832, the only white one remaining in the world. Slowly, he began to play the Intermezzo second movement of "Fantasies," Op 116 by Brahms.

Over the past year, I've learned that he's troubled when Henry plays this melody. Instead of interrupting him, I listened to the sound which seemed to always represent his feelings.

What drove him to play this incredible song? He played every note by heart, each finger instinctively knowing where to go across the keyboard. His fingers danced with magnificent skill over the white and ebony keys. I guessed that he might be upset because I had seen Larry earlier in the week or perhaps it was tomorrow's concert without Katherine singing that troubled him.

For a moment, I closed my eyes entranced by every beautiful note. How blessed I was to be a part of this talented man's life.

Slowly, I walked over to the piano, all my energy focused on the man and the Bosendorfer. A bead of sweat had formed at his temple. With my breasts pressed against his back, I laid my head to rest on his shoulder and gently wiped his brow.

He said nothing, but there was no need for speech. This was his moment to engross himself in what he loved, classical music, and nothing turned me on more than when he played the piano.

"A little Brahms, Songbird?"

"Oh, yes, Brahms," I wanted him to turn around and touch me like he did those keys. With my hair cascading over his shoulder, my hands began to gently massage his neck and shoulders. Breathless and desiring him, I gazed at the side of his handsome face. I noticed every little curve of his cheek as the smell of his aftershave tickled my nose and warmed my body. Every part of me wanted him to turn around and give me the same attention he was giving the instrument.

"This is the second of the 'Fantasies,'" he explained.

I gulped. "Your favorite part."

"My fantasy is that you stay away from Mr. Hillman!" He rose and headed for the door.

I couldn't believe he would get me that dynamic and leave me wanting him so badly. "You're angry?"

He turned. I saw anger in his eyes for the first time in our marriage. "Do you think I should be happy that your ex-boyfriend drove you home, and you didn't tell me?"

"I called for a cab. I didn't know Larry would be my driver," I retorted.

"Well, you should have sent him away."

"I needed a ride home."

"Maybe I should tell you that Betty Redvine hasn't signed the understudy contract yet." He stomped over to me, his eyes seething with rage. "I own that stage, and who sings must remain my decision, never just the Board's."

"I see," I murmured.

"You better be able to live with my decisions, Songbird."

"So, you wouldn't give me the national anthem even if it weren't up to the board?" Tears stung my eyes. This suddenly felt like a betrayal. He wouldn't give me the opportunity after all those voice lessons and music classes. I tried to turn on a heel, but he grabbed my arm stopping me from leaving his side.

"Look at me." He wrapped an arm around my back and pulled me to him. "You aren't ready yet. You have the potential to be as good as Katie or Betty, but you haven't had enough training yet. Do you know what happens to someone when they walk across that stage and aren't properly prepared?"

"I am ready," I countered.

"You think you're ready," he responded. "You want the spotlight, but you don't have enough experience to handle the pressure at this level."

"How dare you!" I pushed out of his hold and ran to the door.

He didn't follow me out of the parlor as I expected. I lay down on the sofa and started to cry. Some of me even wondered if I would ever be as good as Katie or Betty. They both had Bachelor of Music degrees and had been voice teachers for years. I didn't have the same performance experience either. That's true. The truth from the one man whose opinion meant the most to me, cut at my heart. This man made me shiver the moment he walked into the room, like a teenager with a crush. He launched an army of butterflies in my stomach. The most talented man I'd ever met didn't think the same of me.

Suddenly, the door opened, and he entered the room with a coffee mug.

"My favorite sugar-free hot cocoa won't get you out of the doghouse," I warned.

"I was honest," he explained, wiping my tears. "Darling, that doesn't mean that I don't think you're talented, have extreme potential, and don't absolutely adore you. Besides, we don't know how safe things are right now, who hurt Katie and stole Buttercup."

"Buttercup?" I questioned.

"Hiroki's violin has a name, although Hiroki barely uses it because it is too personal. Stradivarius violins are named like children and even numbered. This one was named 'Buttercup' after a flower picked by Hiroki's great, great, great grandfather and given to his great, great, great grandmother. The violin represents their love and is especially unique because it contains a hint of yellow in the varnish which dates to the 1800s."

I sipped the cocoa and realized he had even placed giant marshmallows on top.

"Just the way you like. By the way, you don't know that Katie called the night she was in the hospital and asked that you be the one that took her place in the concert."

"You're kidding?" I couldn't believe it.

"It's true. Katie requested that you perform the national anthem in her place. She didn't know I had mailed Betty the understudy contract last week."

"I see," my tears began to well again. "Betty just hasn't signed it yet."

"You must stop taking these solo appearances personally. You don't understand just how inexperienced you really are; you don't even realize it and that scares me!"

"You're being cruel," I gulped.

"This is my decision. You'll be better prepared after another semester, having sung a few smaller events and with more private voice lessons. I know that you feel I am being hurtful, but I don't want you to go out without much more experience. I'm sorry. I must think what is best for you and your career as a vocalist."

"How about for once you think about what will make your wife happy?"

He grabbed me, and kissed me so passionately that I completely melted in his arms. "As your husband, I must protect you, even from yourself. I will make you happy because that's how you made me."

CHAPTER 27

I hardly saw Henry the next morning. On the day of the performance, he often disappears into the confines of solitude. He'll go for long drives by the Indian River Lagoon to listen to the music he's about to conduct.

About an hour before the concert, I hurried into the walk-in closet and pulled out my favorite black dress. I showered, then slipped on the low-cut gown. For a moment, I debated if I should wear a large hat. In the mirror, I looked at myself. Over the years, I have learned to appreciate being a middle-aged woman. It's rewarding to have feminine curves and still feel sexy at this age.

Quickly, I grabbed a pair of black high-heeled shoes and rushed out the door. Henry had left the Porsche for me; I hurried to sit behind the wheel and drove about ten miles until I approached the Beaumont Auditorium in Palmdale. A valet took my keys and I entered from the side entrance. Behind the giant red curtain, I knew Henry was giving last-minute instructions to the orchestra. I immediately glanced to where I had last seen Katie Croff sprawled on the floor motionless.

A pit formed in my stomach.

Standing by the curtain, Betty Redvine wore a long blue satin and crinoline dress. She waved hello to me, and I returned the kind gesture. Despite deep hidden jealousy, Betty is undoubtedly one of the most talented and beautiful people in Brevard; her beauty is natural, her talent God-given, along with years of master classes by some of the best vocal teachers Julliard had to offer. Her reddish-brown hair sat upon her shoulders in perfectly waved curls. With hardly any make-up, she had no facial flaws.

Suddenly, from behind her, walked Katie Croff. The shock from seeing Katie must have crossed my face.

"You looked surprised," Katie chuckled.

"I thought you weren't going to be here tonight because you are scared," I said.

"I came to cheer Betty on. I'm still not feeling completely 100%, a bit dizzy, so I will stay backstage." Katie grabbed my arm and pulled me aside out of earshot of Betty. Did you hear I told the Big Cheese to give you, my spot?"

"He doesn't think I'm ready," I admitted sadly.

Katie's eyes widened and then tightened. "You still have a few minor timing issues. you need to keep your voice forward with better breath support, but I think you are ready."

I could hardly believe what I was hearing. "You believe in me more than my husband?"

"It could still be the drug," Katie joked.

"You think I'm ready to sing in front of thousands?" I implored.

"The truth is you've impressed me, which kind of says something, doesn't it?"

I didn't know what to say.

"Regardless of Henry's concern, you're still married to one of the most handsome and kind-hearted conductors our world has ever seen," she said. "And it turns out that I am also currently…"

Just then, Henry entered from around the corner, dressed to the nines in a complete, black-vested tuxedo, white dress shirt, and black tie. He glanced at me, grabbed me briefly, and kissed my cheek. "You are sexier than Mozart, Songbird."

Katie laughed, "Why, thank you."

"I think he was talking to his beautiful wife," Betty Redvine chuckled. "Director Coggins, where do you want me to stand?"

"Please excuse me now, Darling. It's time I get to work," Henry then turned toward Betty Redvine. He suddenly raised an elbow for Betty Redvine to take his arm. With a wink back to me, he led Betty toward center stage next to the Director's podium. The audience applause was near deafening as they stood in front of over two thousand spectators inside the sold-out Beaumont Auditorium.

"Break a leg," he spoke to Betty, then stepped onto the podium.

My breath caught in my throat. My husband, the Director of the PSO, was simply magnificent. He patted his chest twice above the heart, which was his way of instructing the orchestra to play passionately.

He raised his baton. Our nation's most excellent song began with a downbeat, the melody that men have lived and died to protect, the "Star Spangled Banner."

Katie Croff suddenly patted my shoulder to interrupt. "I don't mean to stop your ogling over our director, and I'm glad you're not mad at him, but I need to tell you something."

"Don't worry. I'm not going to let the fact my husband doesn't think I'm ready to be a soloist ruin the greatest thing that's ever happened to me, being his wife." I tagged. "He said I'll sing later in the season."

"Actually… you look lovely this evening?" she changed the subject. "That's a gorgeous little black dress. Wherever did you get it? Your trip to Paris over the summer?"

The blonde bombshell with the ample bosom was being way too lovely for a diva, even for her. I turned toward her, ignoring that the audience was standing on their feet and Betty Redvine's perfect voice booming over the speakers.

"Seriously, you look marvelous."

"Katie, what's the matter?" I asked.

"You realize that the missing violin is worth four million dollars?"

"Yes," I glanced at Mr. Hiroki, who played a dark violin instead of the yellow-tinted family legacy. "Are you worried? I know you weren't involved in the violin theft! I was with you in the hospital, remember? I saw how sick you were."

"There's something amiss, but not just the violin theft," Katie shared.

"Ok," I was becoming inquisitive. "What is it?"

"I like you, so this isn't easy." She spoke. "You're a real friend for staying at the hospital for me."

"I'm glad you're feeling better."

"Well, that's a good thing. I hope you still feel like that after I explain something to you," she said. "I haven't been frank about some things."

"Do you know who stole Mr. Hiroki's violin?" I asked. "Did you remember someone snatching the violin out of the case?"

"No, but I know why your ex-boyfriend Larry Hillman was in the taxi outside that night. Larry was held for questioning last night by the police and I wanted you to know he's not stalking you."

"What?"

"How can I put this? I honestly think your ex...well... he's a real cat's pajamas," she added.

"A cat's...what?"

From out of the shadows, Larry Hillman slowly padded over to stand behind me. "She's trying to tell you we've been dating for a few months," Larry explained. "I wanted to tell you myself but didn't know how you would take it."

As the high note during "Land of the Free" signaled the end of the national anthem, I asked loudly, "You are dating, Larry?"

Katie smiled. "What can I say? I got a thing for cab drivers?"

"Cab drivers?" I gasped.

"It must be the little name tag," Katie grinned. "You okay with this?"

Larry Hillman wrapped his arm around the one woman who seemed to have it all: talent and beauty. The pit in my stomach grew but I realized it wasn't envy --just surprise.

"Yeah, I'm fine," I mumbled.

"This is a lot to take in," Katie said.

"Is there anything else?"

"Yes, there's more," Katie admitted.

Larry leaned in and whispered in my ear. "Katie thinks your husband stole Mr. Hiroki's Stradivarius, and we want you to help us prove it."

As the horror of what they were thinking triggered immediate trembling down my spine, I heard over two thousand suddenly applauding. The song had ended. Quickly, I turned to see my husband graciously raising a hand toward Betty for everyone to clap for her. A few seconds passed, and then he reached over to take the microphone with Betty bowing gracefully. As she began to walk off stage from the ovation, Henry greeted the audience, "Good evening, Ladies and Gentlemen. Welcome to Rouse and Vivaldi

"Impossible," I gasped. "Henry had nothing to do with Mr. Hiroki's missing Stradivarius! I saw him standing right on the podium when you collapsed."

Larry announced, "Your husband could be behind the sale."

"You've had it in for Henry from the beginning," I chided.

"You're right. I think you deserve better," Larry sighed deeply as Betty Redvine strode by. "He makes you feel less than you really are. I think your voice is a Rolls Royce."

I smiled, "I'm fine, and thank you."

"I'm not buttering your biscuit here, Maria. You've got pizazz regardless of what Henry thinks. You know the playhouse is doing *Fiddler on the Roof.* You should try out and join me. Maybe you'll get a lead role!"

"I'm super busy with Music Theory and classical voice training this college semester," I reminded.

"Fiddlesticks," Katie said.

"Classical training? That came out of the mouth of the rock-in-roll queen of Black Widow. Can you believe this?" Larry shook his head. "A few months as a Director's wife, she thinks she's too good to sing rock or perform theater."

"That's just not true! I love all musical forms," I retorted. "It's not that I think I'm any better. You need to open your eyes, Larry, and see that I love opera and find it challenging."

"Don't ever think performing musical theater isn't challenging! Theater folk works their asses off! We dance, sing, and act. If you ask me, your college classes are easier than performing live musical theater night after night," Katie pressed.

"I'm sorry," I responded to Katie. "I didn't mean to offend you. Musical theater has the best songs and stories in all the world. And I know how hard you work, Katie. You've earned my respect for all you've done, but opera is where my voice fits best, and I love singing Italian arias."

The crowd began to sit, and the cheers muted as Henry spoke over the P.A. microphone system, "Music is the world's most cherished universal language. More than that, music is my best friend, a friend I want to share with you all tonight." I heard through the monitor on the left.

Turning toward Larry, Maria said, "Please stop making up stories about the man I love."

Larry grabbed my shoulders and looked me directly in the eyes. "Before the PSO, your husband worked part-time for Art & Music Gallery, and three valuable musical instruments were reported missing."

"I am not even sure Henry ever worked for a gallery. When we started dating, I told Henry his past remains in the past."

Katie interrupted. "His past includes having a reputation as a playboy and being dishonest with women. Even I know that."

"That was before we dated," I reminded. Not wanting to hear more, I turned to listen to my husband speak.

"Other than music, my one true love is my new lovely wife, Marie. In honor of being happily married these past three months, I'd like to play a song just for her, a little Mozart," The orchestra began to play the First Movement of *Eine Kleine Nachtmusik.* Henry appeared breathtakingly handsome, attracting me from where he stood in the front center of the orchestra. He controlled every section with just a simple movement of his wrists. Oh, what amazing hands he has!

"I thought they would start the Vivaldi's Four Seasons concert. 'Spring,' right?" Katie questioned.

"'Spring' is the encore song," my husband glanced at me and smiled. My heart warmed with the slight curve of his cheeks. With a wink, he returned his attention to the orchestra and continued with solid precision. "This is *Eine Kleine Nachtmusik* or *A Little Night Music.* It's our Mozart serenade," I informed Katie. "When I first met Henry, he wasn't really a fan of this particular composition by Mozart but because I love it so much, now he thinks of me and doesn't dislike it any longer."

"Oh," Katie blushed.

"Well, he's a romantic thief," Larry said.

I reassured. "My husband is a man of integrity."

Larry shook his head no. "I know a lot about your husband. When I heard you married him, I hired a detective to learn who Henry Coggins is. I learned things you would never want to know."

Suddenly, Katie shouted. "Excuse you? You hired who? Okay, I stand corrected. My boyfriend is stalking you."

"Beethoven's a thief," Larry explained. "He even spent a night in jail, released only because the cops couldn't find enough evidence on the missing musical instruments."

"Perhaps you are the one who steals and tries to blame it on my husband," I interrupted.

"You know me better than that!" Larry argued.

"I know Henry better than you," I gulped. "We must concentrate on finding the real thief and the person who hurt Katie! Do you have any enemies, Katie?"

"Unless you call the cable company who just found out I didn't report getting free HBO."

"I doubt that would be the cause," I smiled. "You stole HBO?"

"I wouldn't recommend it," Katie said. "It was quite embarrassing."

"All right," Larry snipped. "The PSO is missing a five-million-dollar violin. Out of all of us, other than my girlfriend's HBO crisis, your husband is the only one with a questionable background in musical instrument theft."

"You're wrong about Henry," I said. "What about Karl or the timpani player, that Charlie McDaniels?"

Katie whirled around to stare at the robust man behind the giant timpani drums. "I'm pretty sure I wouldn't have missed all that red hair coming toward me that night."

Larry interrupted. "I may have even figured out who might be handling the violin deal on the black market. Now I need your help, Maria. Are you in or out?"

"In proving my husband is a criminal! I'm out!"

"Okay, then let me put it this way. How would you like to help Katie and me solve this so that your husband doesn't go to jail for the rest of his life for the grand thief and attempted murder."

"Well, when you put it that way," I paused. "I'm in just to prove you all wrong."

CHAPTER 29

Jennifer Miller started to cry. She grabbed onto the wall to stop herself from fainting. Heather immediately put down her paranormal equipment and rushed to help her. Bradly removed his headphones and rushed to help Jennifer, who seemed shocked.

The two helped her out of the music library and walked her over to sit at her desk.

"Leave our librarian alone, Uncle Max!" After seeing Jennifer was now safe in the chair, Bradly slammed the library door.

Immediately, bangs could be heard from the other side of the door. It was as if the filing cabinets were opening and closing. Jennifer's tearing eyes widened in horror.

"Having a temper tantrum," Bradly surmised.

Heather sat down in the chair in front of Jennifer's desk. "Are you all right?"

Jennifer took a few deep breaths as Bradly came to stand by Jennifer's side, handing her a tissue. "It looks like the haunting is attached to you."

"Oh my God!" Jennifer continued to cry. She placed her nose into the Kleenex and blew. "I can't believe this!"

"Can you tell us about your Uncle Max?" Heather asked.

Bradly grabbed a chair and carried it over to sit next to Jennifer. He began to rub her arm in comfort. For a teenager who looked like he belonged at a Metalhead concert, he was caring and appeared very concerned.

"Thank you," Jennifer said when he handed her the Kleenex box.

"This Uncle Max must be a nasty guy," Bradly said.

"You have no idea," Jennifer sniffled and somehow maintained composure. "This is such a shock. Now that I think about it, the haunting did begin after my uncle died and I took this job."

"Would that upset him? You are working here?"

"No, not really. He was a music teacher and soloist for the PSO many times. Oh, and he loved Mozart. So that's why he keeps knocking over the Mozart bust; he wanted me to know it was him."

Bradly stopped rubbing her arm. "Please, you need to tell us everything you can about your uncle so we can send him into the light, and he'll leave you alone then and stop haunting the library."

"Oh, this is hard." Jennifer sat up in the chair. "Should I even talk about it here? Maybe my uncle can hear. I will have to quit if we can't get rid of him. My Uncle Max is an evil man."

"Not a nice ghost either." Bradly snipped.

"I think you should be fine talking here. She looked at her meter. It's not picking up any disturbances out here." Heather said.

"Okay, if that thing starts beeping. I am going to stop

talking about him. Deal?" Jennifer glanced over at Bradly.

"Deal," Bradly said. "Tell us as much as you can."

"My Uncle was a music teacher married to my father's sister. The family liked him at first. He seemed like a good provider, and he loved classical music. He started working at Hibiscus Cove High School. It went well, and so did their marriage for about ten years. Then, when I became a teen and started going to that school. No one knew he was my uncle, and I started hearing rumors that he was sleeping with a cheerleader. Her name was Mary, and she was quite beautiful, blonde, skinny, and came from money."

"Oh no!" Heather gasped. "Was it true?"

"I went into his classroom after band class to confront him. I walked in and saw them kissing. I screamed in horror and told my aunt what I had seen that afternoon. I realize now, with maturity, I probably should have dealt with it more silently, maybe demanding they stop instead of ruining his marriage myself."

"This is awful!" Heather gasps. "Did your aunt divorce him?"

"No," Jennifer cried. "She hung herself in the master bedroom after sending a letter to the high school. My Uncle lost his wife and his job in the same week."

"He blamed you," Bradly said.

"Yes," Jennifer nodded.

"Did he threaten or hurt you?" Bradly asked.

"Worse," Jennifer said. "He would follow me as I walked

to school in his car. He liked to stalk me, and my parents had to put a restraining order on him. It was so bad my father was still getting over the loss of his sister and then he had to deal with her adulterous crazy man."

"That must have devasted your father."

"For two years, my father hardly spoke to me. It took us going into counseling for him to realize that her mental illness caused her death more than me. She suffered from depression from time to time. They realized my aunt had stopped taking her medicine for over a week before she had hanged herself. The police had counted the pills and did a blood test to confirm that she had stopped taking her medicine, and I gave her information she couldn't handle." Jennifer sniffled. "I still blame myself. Now, he won't even leave me alone after his death."

"Did he die by suicide, too?" Bradly questioned.

"No," Jennifer breathed. "He left me alone after the order and never spoke to my parents again. We found out in the obituary that he had died of a heart attack."

"Heart," Jennifer said.

"Her uncle may not be mentally stable either," Bradly said.

"He never was. My father always blamed him for my aunt's depression. She didn't have issues until she married him."

Jennifer looked over at Bradly. "This is bad. We may need to bring in a Priest right away. He may be here for revenge?"

CHAPTER 30

"What a concert, Maestro! Four standing ovations! A grand night for Vivaldi, Rouse, and the audience loved *A Little Night Music* thrown in at the beginning for grandeur," exclaimed Dr. Jeffry Landers.

"We haven't had a concert like that since Harvard," Charles McDaniels reminded Henry, "It must have been all the press about the missing violin. The audience was just so enthusiastic."

I overheard Charlie McDaniels' compliment as I entered the foyer. Four of the most prestigious men in Brevard, the PSO Board members, were sitting around the twelve-foot dining table. The fifth was the only female on the board, press, and PR expert, Judy.

In my hand was a tray of coffee cups and a hot pot of coffee; slowly, I walked around the table, placing a cup in front of each guest.

"It was a great evening," Henry shook the doctor's hand. "I'm all ready to start working on Beethoven's Fifth in the spring."

"Were you able to hire a special pianist for the "Moonlight Sonata?" Dr. Landers asked.

Henry admitted. "I've invited David Wilson to play the 'Sonata in C-sharp Minor.'"

"The concert will surely sell out with David's reputation."

Walking around the table, I filled the coffee cups for each

guest. Checking that half of the pastries had been eaten, I noticed the bear claw was gone. Knowingly, I smiled at Henry. Bear claws were his favorite, and somehow, he managed to snag the only claw.

"Thank you," Henry smiled as I filled his coffee mug.

"I was surprised that your wife didn't sing the national anthem. Katie Croff informed me that she specially requested Maria to sing as her replacement," Judy commented sternly.

Stopping in my tracks, I wondered how Henry would reply. Briefly, I glanced at him wide-eyed as he nearly dropped his mug. "Thank you," I commented softly.

"Don't worry," Henry said. "I understand my wife has an amazing voice and is adored by many. I've asked Katie to start giving my wife private lessons on stage presence and performance."

I glanced over at him wide-eyed and very pleased. "Thank you," I repeated.

"I was going to speak to Maria privately, but I want the board to know that my wife has the potential to be a world-class vocalist, and she will be a star performer with the PSO. I want her to have a solid foundation, the best performance, and vocal training available."

Tears stung my eyes. I quickly nodded at him and hurried out of the room, knowing he indeed believed in me. It would have seemed like the happiest moment in my life if it hadn't been for Larry and Katie's suspicion that Henry was involved in the disappearance of Mr. Hiroki's precious violin.

I eavesdropped just outside the door as Henry passed

creamer and ate his breakfast pastry.

Judy continued. "The PSO must remember that voice is an instrument, too. The people surely love their grand singers. It is well noted that your wife is an up-and-comer."

"Don't forget about "B" Rohecli, Liza, Kossa, and Conland; they should also be included in next year's line-up as vocalists. I'm deciding if the PSO should host 'A Night at The Opera.'"

"What a splendid idea!" Kevin Mason agreed. "Voice is an instrument that must be celebrated! Next season what about *Carmina Burana* by Carl Orff with a grand chorus."

"Mendelsohn," argued Judy. "We should do *Elijah* and star them. We could get James Noggleminodolph as Elijah!"

"*Elijah*, do we dare! And Noggleminodolph, he's so expensive!" Kevin Mason added. "That is quite an undertaking. And I must say only someone with Henry's conducting skills would ever even attempt to direct such a difficult masterpiece. Would you even consider it?"

"*Elijah*, of course! Bach has some great oratorios as well. These are all exceptional, and I would love to conduct them all if you all will give me a moment through today. Instead of starting to plan the next season, I see a critical need in our community. I want to put back on the table my idea of several free concerts a year to allow everyone the chance to attend some of the PSO events throughout the season," Henry explained.

Suddenly, the room drew silent. The board had always shot down Henry's attempts to make the orchestra more publicly accessible to those who couldn't afford the one-to-two-hundred-dollar tickets.

"Now, Henry, you know how I felt about this when you mentioned it several months ago," Doctor Landers grimaced. "The symphony is elite because of our strict sales and..."

"What about the children?" my husband interrupted. "We need to promote symphony music. They are growing up without being able to listen to the world's great composers. These children are the future of music."

"Are you going to expose them to the Elfking?" laughed Judy. "Perhaps a little *Requiem, Dies Irae*; all the mothers surely will love us for that."

"Not all symphony music is lighthearted because a composer's life isn't always kind. I'll pick appropriate pieces to share the PSO's love of classical music with those who may have never been exposed to live symphony music." Henry pressed. "I want to inspire children to join their school bands, choirs, ensembles and take lessons. They just aren't being exposed to enough orchestra music because the prices of our tickets keep going up."

"I have to say, Henry," Dr. Landers added, "the main reason we have maintained such a loyal audience is the difficulty of getting PSO tickets."

I peeked in through the cracked open door. Henry had risen, traveled down the hall, and opened the front door of our house. In came a boy about the age of thirteen and an elderly woman. "Then you give me no choice," Henry turned away to the newcomers. "Come join us, please."

"We have guests. I thought this was a closed board meeting," Judy said.

"Let our guests speak," Charlie McDaniels countered. "I want to hear more about Henry's FREE concert idea."

"Tell them who you are, Jason," Henry told the young boy.

"My name is Jason Luther," he said. "Mr. Coggins asked me to be here to tell you that I have never heard you guys play before."

"Why not?" Henry asked him.

"My dad left us so my mom says the PSO is too much money."

"Do you play anything?" Henry inquired.

"The violin. I am first chair in my Junior High school orchestra."

"Have you ever heard a professional live symphony before?" Henry asked.

"No, but I've wanted to. My Mom says there is nothing like it in the whole world."

Henry smiled. "There isn't. Thank you for coming, Jason."

"Okay, my ride is waiting outside and I'm late for soccer," he hurried out the door.

"And you, Madam, who are you, and why are you here?"

"My name is Rosa Dean, and I am seventy-two years old and a retired hairdresser. I'm on Social Security and a very fixed income with lots of medical bills. I am here to tell you that I have wanted to go to the symphony for the past five years, and I have never been able to go except for the one time you did that Christmas program at that Methodist church on the beach. All those Christmas hymns played by the orchestra brought tears to my eyes."

"Yes, God is in the music," Henry agreed.

"Indeed," Rosa smiled up at him. "And you're a hunk." She winked at him.

Henry laughed, "Thank you and we appreciate your time coming this morning to speak to the board."

"It says in the Bible, right there in Psalms 150. Praise the Lord! Praise him with trumpet sound; praise him with lute and harp! Praise him with timbrel and dance; praise him with strings and pipe! Praise him with sounding cymbals; praise him with loud clashing cymbals! Let everything that breathes praise the Lord! Praise the Lord!" Rosa added. "Jesus didn't want people to stop praising God because of ticket prices, nor should the PSO."

The entire board watched wide-eyed as Rosa turned and slowly left the room.

Henry snatched a paper-filled folder in front of him on the table. "Hundreds of letters from children, college students, and seniors who can't afford our tickets! One was from a man who lost his leg fighting in WWII. If you excuse me for a moment, I'll be back shortly. I am asking the Board to reconsider my request or consider hiring another Director for the PSO."

"Did I just hear you correctly?" Dr. Spencer Macy, the scientist, gasped.

"I am not asking. I am demanding several events a year

to be given for FREE. During the season, we should apply major discounts for students, teachers, veterans, and seniors."

Suddenly, Dr. Landers burst into a hearty laugh. "And how can the PSO afford to do that? Do you know the cost of putting on a symphony concert? This is ridiculous!"

I peeked around the corner only to see the redness enter my husband's cheeks. He was livid that, again, his idea of free concerts seemed to be rejected by board members. Henry Coggins considered one of the most talented orchestra directors in the world, stormed out of the room in a huff. I even wondered, as those sitting around the table silenced, if he would return to the meeting at all.

CHAPTER 31

I followed Henry down the hallway as he approached his private study. Patiently, I stood outside, wondering if I should knock. Suddenly, the door cracked open, and Henry stood in the doorway staring down at me.

"Are you all, right?" I asked.

"I wanted to make my point to the Board," Henry said.

"It certainly was made," I replied.

Henry took a step aside, "Come in."

My husband's private study is always a mess. Sheet music and science fiction novels lay stacked against every wall. Beside one giant beige recliner in front of massive speakers stood a music stand. This is where Henry went to study music or read; this was his space, his "man cave."

"The PSO Board needs to respect how much I want to inspire kids," he explained.

"They certainly do now," I commented.

"Do you agree with me?" he asked.

"Yes, I do," I admitted.

"I still shouldn't have threatened to quit."

"You've got to do what you feel is necessary." I moved closer to him.

Suddenly, he grabbed me, leaned in and gently kissed my

lips. His arms wrapped around me. I felt my knees quake and my body press against his massive frame.

The kiss broke, and when I glanced up, there was a big smile on his handsome face. "You're right," he concluded.

"So, are you going to return to the meeting?" I wondered aloud.

"I could just skip the rest, and we make our own music."

"Sounds grand," I grinned.

"I should at least say good-bye, perhaps for the last time to the board." Henry released me and stormed down the hallway and into the room with the PSO Board.

"Henry, you can't quit the PSO. I won't hear of it." Judy demanded as he walked in. "Please be aware that the PSO comprises many music teachers. If you look at the big picture here, you'll see offering free music concerts could hurt many professionals in our music community, just like with music lessons. If someone offers lessons for free, then those private music teachers who charge will go out of business. No music is ever free. We've all paid for lessons and music education so why pretend it should be?"

"I disagree," Charlie McDaniels interrupted. "Not only is it exclusive for those who can't afford our tickets but even for those who can. A few free concerts could even bring us a larger audience that will eventually buy tickets. Some might try a few of our concerts, realize how much fun they are, and purchase season passes."

"All right, I don't want to hear anything like the word 'quit' from our great Maestro ever again. Henry, we'll put your free concert idea in writing and the board will take a vote on it at next month's meeting," Dr. Landers announced.

Judy interrupted. "There are many pros and cons that must fully be considered, especially the effects, including the fact that people may wait to come to our free concerts instead of paying for tickets."

"I understand your concerns," Henry admitted.

"Then you see you do have some serious hurdles getting my vote," Judy added.

"I've heard all the arguments but that still doesn't change the fact that there are so many children, veterans, teachers and seniors who can't afford to attend," my husband stated. "They deserve to be here."

"I understand, Maestro," Judy rose from her seat. "You certainly have made us think about how seriously you want this. I am sure that none of us wish you to go."

"The future of this PSO symphony maybe those kids out there who can't afford to come." He added, "Growing up with a single mother, I was one of those teenage players in my junior high band. I used to want to go so badly to a symphony concert, but my mother couldn't afford to take me. So, I would sneak out at night and listen outside the Beaumont building. My mother found me there once, but instead of yelling at me for sneaking out the window, she cried. She promised me that one day I would never have to worry about the price of a ticket again. My instrument and talent would earn me a college scholarship and a degree. My mother was right. Now that I am a Doctor of Music and the PSO Maestro, it's my turn to worry about the children who can't afford to sit in the Beaumont."

Dr. Landers concluded. "We'll vote at our next meeting, Maestro. Please let's continue."

"Not today, Dr. Landers. Please let yourselves out. I've got rehearsal tonight and a lot on my mind with this investigation." The second the last member left the house, Henry shuffled down the hallway to reenter the man cave.

Quickly, he took me in his arms and kissed my lips, ever so tenderly.

"I'm so proud of you," I announced, as he sent chills down my spine. "You stood up for what you believed in."

"Symphony music will never be just for some," his hands went to the back of my dress and slowly unzipped the back as my clothes fell to the floor, and I stood there naked in front of him. He continued to kiss every part of me, and I lost my breath, nearly falling to the floor.

Quickly, he raised me and placed me on the chair.

"On top of the Bosendorfer," I asked, "or do you have something else in mind?"

"No need to clean off the piano," his hands pulled me closer as my long red nails suddenly gripped his shoulders.

And together, what beautiful music we made!

CHAPTER 32

Gardening is a pastime joy for me. Since moving into my husband's beachside estate, I'd spent many beautiful evenings watering a small garden and caring for my favorite sunflowers in our yard that overlooks the sea.

It was a tradition in my family to care even for flowers. My grandfather Tom grew sunflowers for my grandmother Margaret every summer, and from then on, the practice began: growing sunflowers to give to those you love. To me, the sunflowers are so beautiful; it's proof of how unique God's creation is.

The sea breeze was cool tonight as the glowing sun began to set. I could hear Henry playing piano from an open window. He wasn't playing an entire song but bits and pieces, repeating certain sections, perhaps he was writing a new composition, I surmised, tilting my watering can.

Noticing one brilliant sunflower by the fence, I moved over to make sure I watered the plant deeply. As I leaned over, I felt something hard pressing against the back of my spine.

Whatever it was pinched me, and I whirled around to face the barrel of a gun.

I'd never been so close to a gun before. Shockingly, I couldn't move. I felt my mouth gape open, staring at it, pointed now directly at my chest.

He said, "Don't say a word."

Slowly, I glanced up to face the intruder. He was a small

man of Asian descent. Well dressed in a suit, I didn't expect a criminal to dress so fashionably.

I wanted to ask him who he was and what he wanted, but all I could do was blink. From a distance, I could hear Henry softly playing. All I had to do was scream, just let out one of those curdling screeches.

"Scream," I thought.

"Just scream."

Instead, the heavy watering can be dropped from my fingers, landing directly on the man's foot. He let out a yelp, grabbed his left big toe, and started hopping on one foot. Suddenly, I realized this was an opportunity to run, so I did.

I ran for the back doors to find Henry opening them. He didn't look at all worried until he saw my face. Then he took a step out as I tried to catch my breath. Instead of speaking, I pushed him inside and locked the glass doors, huffing and puffing.

"What's wrong? Are you hurt?" he gasped.

"There's…a…. man…with…" I rushed to the glass door to see if he was still in the garden.

Breathing deeply to calm myself, I still fell to my knees.

Henry suddenly dropped. "Do you need me to call 9-1-1? You look like you've seen a ghost."

I took three deep breaths and finally could say, "There was a little man with a gun in our garden. He said not to scream but I dropped a watering can on his toe and managed to escape."

"A watering can be your weapon of choice?" Then, as quickly as he had asked, he rushed toward the shelves and pulled a gun from behind a music stand.

"A gun is better. Stay here," he ordered, then he rushed out the door.

What the hell is happening? I thought to myself. Does Henry own a gun? I sat there on the floor, wondering what I should do. Should I run after my husband and tell him to stay inside? I didn't want him to defend me; I wanted him alive more.

Getting the courage to stand, I rushed to the door, but he had returned. "Whoever it was is gone now."

"You own a gun?" I asked my husband.

"It's my father's," he admitted. "He was in the army and into handguns. I got it down from the attic after what happened to Katie."

I plopped onto the sofa and said, "We need to call the police."

"Yes," he agreed. "We'll fill out a report. It's probably best if we don't stay here tonight."

"I'll pack us a bag." I offered.

"Enough for a few days; let's get out of town until the police figure this out." He spoke. "The Orlando Jazz Symphony is doing a tribute to Benny Goodman and we might as well go because I need to meet with the band leader."

"Sing, Sing, Sing' is one of my all-time favorites. Sounds wonderful."

"Don't know if we'll have time to do the swing, but we'll be safe enough if no one knows where to find us." He wrapped his arms around me. "Songbird, I'm guessing whoever that is thinks one of us stole the Stradivarius."

"But you wouldn't do that," I exclaimed.

"There are many things you don't know," he said coldly. "Things I wish I could change about myself, but it is too late now. I want to keep you safe at all costs. That means we'll have to go away for a while."

"Can we afford to do that?"

"Oh, we are quite rich at the moment." He announced.

Suddenly, I wondered if he had something to do with that stolen violin. Mr. Hiroki is Asian on his mother's side. Was this some act of revenge for the stolen violin?

"I'll explain on the way to O' town."

Quickly, I trotted up to the bedroom filled with two suitcases of clothes and toiletries we might use for the trip. I hurried into the parlor. Before I could step out, he grabbed them from me, took out his gun, and said, "I'll put these in the trunk and pull right up to the door."

Henry hurried to the Porsche, loaded the trunk, spun the car entirely in the front driveway, and drove nearly up the stoop. Henry was wrecking my sunflowers, but I decided not to complain.

"Get in," he yelled.

Suddenly, I heard a shot as I stood in the doorway. Splinters of wooden doors nearly four inches from my face brushed my cheeks. I ducked and heard more gunfire.

Henry climbed out the side window and began shooting across the street at what looked like a luxury SUV and the little man who had been in my garden. I couldn't believe that this was happening.

The phone started ringing as the two men continued to exchange gunfire. I realized the phone was only a few feet away. I ducked and reached for it.

"Hello, help, please call 9-1-1. My husband and I are getting shot at in our home. Please!"

"This is GBS pharmacy. Your prescription is ready for pickup. Thank you for your order and choosing GBS pharmacy," said the recorded voice.

I slammed down the phone and quickly dialed 9-1-1.

"Hello, is this an emergency?"

The gunfire continued. "Hello, are you being shot at?" the dispatch operator inquired.

"This is Mrs. Coggins on Plumeria Road, 454 Plumeria. Yes, we are being shot at. My husband is holding off a gunman trying to kill us."

"Police are on their way," she said. "What can you tell us about the gunman? How many?"

"One, and he's wearing a nice suit."

"Define nice," she asked.

"It's got three large designer buttons down the front and pinstriped. I'm guessing a European designer because he is a smaller man with huge hands considering his size."

Suddenly, Henry rushed back inside and slammed the door. "I'm out of ammo!"

"I'm on the phone with the police," I announced.

"Good," he said.

Then, suddenly, there was gunfire near the door. Henry grabbed me, and I dropped the phone in one swoop. He lifted me off the ground, carrying me to the man cave hallway. He locked the door.

I realized then that we were in the only room with no windows.

"We can't get out now," I gasped.

"We're safe in here." He spoke. "This is a hurricane shelter with a bulletproof lock. Twelve-inch steel is between us and him now. Now all we must do is wait until the police come."

I plopped down on the chair where we had made such fantastic love just last night. Suddenly, I realized that Larry had been right; I didn't know my husband –or even my own house.

CHAPTER 33

With every bullet that dented the door, I winced in fear that the man cave wouldn't hold back the gunman. "The police are on their way!"

Suddenly, Henry stuffed his gun underneath his belt and grabbed my hand. "We're not going to stay." In two steps, he held the television remote. He pressed several buttons and suddenly the glass skylight slid to the right, leaving an opening at the top of the ten-foot ceiling.

"No worries," he pressed another button, and suddenly a long rope with a small loop at the end, dropped from the right side of the skylight. He stuck his patent leather shoe in the loop and then grabbed me. "You might want to put your arms around me."

A part of me didn't want to. I wondered if I should go any further with this apparent "stranger" or wait for the police. I glanced at the door being dented by bullets.

"Are you coming with me or not?" he demanded.

"I don't even know you," I softly responded.

"You know I love you," he smiled.

There was something in his eyes, a look that I'd never seen before, which seemed to gaze deeply into my very soul. Henry could melt with one glance; all he had to do was smile and I was putty.

"No rush," he said sarcastically. "Gunman. Police. I'll wait."

I wrapped my arms around his neck and tightened my grasp. One hand grasped at my back, pushing my body tightly against his. His other fingers took the rope and then we rose like Princess Leila and Luke from *Star Wars*. Henry reeled us upward directly to the sunroof in a daring escape. Once we reached the roof, we were pulled over the ledge until we both lay on top of the tiles.

"Follow me," he commanded as he quickly rose.

Wondering if I even should, I traversed after Henry over the roof to the garage. Listening, I could still hear the gunman shooting at the man-cave door. The gunman had no clue that we had already escaped. In the distance, I began to hear the oncoming sirens of the police.

As we approached the garage, I noticed a latch and what looked like an entrance from the roof. He pressed another button on his remote and an opening appeared, allowing entrance to the garage below.

Over the edge, I saw that stairs had dropped down, allowing us easy access to the vehicles below. I couldn't believe that all this spy-like equipment had been in my house all this time.

I wanted to feel guilty about not knowing this was here, but then I concluded most women don't walk on their roofs looking for hidden entrances. This wasn't my stupidity, I realized. Henry had been hiding so much from me; I felt this was just the beginning.

"Where are we going?" I asked.

"I have something to show you," he took two stairs at a time until we reached the dark garage. He walked past the

Lexus and BMW SUV without turning on a light. He pushed at what looked like some corkboard holding many power tools. Suddenly, the door dropped to the floor, revealing a secret part of the garage. Behind it wasn't a fancy sports car with super speed –but a small, beige, four-door Chevy Chevette.

My eyes searched his with utter surprise. The Chevette was the car I had owned in my early twenties. This, of course, wasn't the same one; I had run that Chevette into the ground to the point the doors were welded shut and rusty holes dotted the floorboards.

"This is the same model as my very first car!" I smiled.

"It is your Christmas gift," he admitted. "Remember when I asked you what your favorite car was? I expected to hear something like a Lamborghini, but you said it was your Chevy instead. I thought I would buy you another Chevette as a memento of times past."

"That was very thoughtful," I hurried over to it, stroking the tiny doors. "How did you ever find one? Chevy stopped making these cars decades ago."

"It's from Nevada. There was an older woman who just left it in her garage for about twenty years. She never drove it and it never got rained on, so it looks and runs beautifully."

"This is so not your style," I replied.

"Yes, I am more of a Porsche man, but I learned along life's journey that people can cherish items that aren't of financial value."

"I love it!" I fought the tears welling up in my eyes.

"Good," he opened the front door and handed me the keys. "Now, drive away. Once I open the garage door, hit the gas pedal, and leave. Your car has been upgraded, so it's a little faster than the one you had long ago."

"What about you?"

"Don't worry about me," he said. "Call a cab at the corner of 5th and Main Street. Larry is expecting you to call."

"I don't understand," I retorted.

"Larry will protect you until I can handle the current situation."

"Who was the gunman?" I inquired.

"I honestly don't know," Henry admitted softly.

"Is he related to Mr. Hiroki in some way?" For a moment, I searched Henry's eyes. He was unreadable as he held the door open. I was afraid to go without him. Regardless of the lies, I still had feelings for him.

"I'm not leaving without you," I argued.

"From now on, being with me will be dangerous."

"I am not leaving without you," I repeated. "You are my husband, and I will not go."

He slammed the car door shut, bent down, and fervently kissed my lips.

CHAPTER 34

I saw the sparkle in his eyes. It reminded me of the very first time I saw him at that fundraiser for music students at the college. There was something very special about Henry; I am undeniably attracted to this man, and I have an unstoppable desire to have him forever in my arms.

Suddenly, the door of the garage opened, and I whirled around screaming. What I found wasn't the gunman --it was Larry. Katie was standing beside him in a leather pantsuit and carrying a rifle.

I barely believed what I was seeing. I gasped, "Why are you two here? Why are you dressed like Catwoman?"

"No time to explain. We were going to a Comics event," Larry said, jumping into the side seat of the Chevette. Katie got in behind him.

Quickly, I glanced over to Henry, who nodded for me to get in the back seat with Katie. "No, I'll drive," Henry said.

"Good thinking because Maria has a lead foot," Larry laughed.

Henry grabbed the keys and I got into the backseat next to Katie. Henry slid behind the wheel and steered the Chevette out of the garage. We left the gunman running in the dust. As we sped out of the driveway, Henry took Katie's rifle and shot out the gunman's back tire.

"Smart thinking," Larry said.

"Good. I wasn't sure we could outrun him in this car,"

Katie snickered.

"Don't be so sure," Henry smiled.

Larry suddenly leaned around to stare at Henry as the Chevette rolled onto the interstate. "You headed to Orlando, right?"

"I should have known you'd be watching the house, Larry. Do you think my husband is capable of stealing Hiroki's violin? You're blaming Henry for what happened to Katie, too," I said.

"I'm worried about you too," Larry glared at Henry. "I know all about what happened in Miami."

Henry didn't flinch. "You know that I spent some time in jail, then?"

Larry had been right. "So, you did go to jail?" I asked my husband. "For what and how long?"

"I paid for a crime I didn't even do," Henry responded.

Exhaling a breath, I realized why Larry and Katie had been so sure Henry had been involved in the theft of Mr. Byrd's precious violin worth millions of dollars.

"You may not have taken it yourself, but we want to know who helped you. We figured you masterminded the entire theft," Katie added. "And if you did, I don't appreciate being drugged, Henry."

"What was stolen years ago that landed you in jail?" I asked, bringing the Chevette to 80 miles an hour, swerving between traffic.

"It's a long story," he placed his hand on my shoulder.

"I've learned the hard way that a person can't live their life looking in the rearview mirror. I'm a changed man whose focus and life are in front of me, with you."

"All this cover-up of your past," I said, gazing at him through the window. "Do I even know you?"

"You know me enough," he announced.

Larry faced the windshield. "So, you do love her?"

"That isn't even in question," Henry said.

"What about Deana, the piano player?" Katie suddenly belted out. "I saw you pulling her aside after your last PSO rehearsal."

Henry pulled the Chevette over. With a skid of the tires, the vehicle nearly lost half the rubber off its tires.

I shouted at her, not wanting to hear the next thing out of Katie's mouth. "Are you telling me not only is my husband an ex-con, but he's also cheating on me with the PSO pianist?"

"Deana is a high-end prostitute," Katie said. "Everyone in the symphony knows what she does for a living."

"Is that why you love to have sex with me on top of the piano?" I asked him. "Is she the source of your piano fetish?"

"Wow, too much information!" Larry pulled the Spiderman ball cap further down on his shaved head. "You never had sex with me on any piano, Marie. There is even one in my grandma's house."

"You would have insisted on top of a drum set," I retorted. "You're into rock-n-roll, remember?"

Larry belted out a laugh.

Katie reminded. "Larry's drumstick is all mine now."

"I only kept Deana after rehearsal because she was playing Rachmaninoff's Prelude in G Minor too staccato," Henry explained. "Every note in op. 23 needs to be heard. Regardless of my past, I did not steal Hiroki's Stradivarius or proposition Deana. She is one of the best pianists in the county, regardless of her extracurricular activities. I am happily married now."

"Happily, is it?" I gulped.

Suddenly, out of the corner of my eye, I saw in the side-view mirror an SUV pulling behind the Chevette. Behind the wheel was Mr. Hiroki. He got out of his van and started walking over with his cane.

"Should I restart the engine?"

Henry opened the back door of the car. "I'll deal with him myself."

"Keep my rifle," Katie said. "Your violinist probably thinks you were involved in the theft like the rest of us."

Henry tossed Katie's weapon back in the back seat, moved his jacket, and showed he was carrying his gun.

"Beethoven is dangerous after all," Larry said, sneering. "You never listened to me when we dated, Maria, and you still don't listen."

As Henry walked toward Mr. Hiroki, I suddenly remembered, "Henry's gun is out of bullets."

CHAPTER 35

Shivers ran down my spine. I didn't want Henry to face Mr. Hiroki, especially if he could be behind the gunfire back at the mansion.

As Mr. Hiroki approached Henry with a stern expression on his face, I exited the Chevette.

"I should apologize to you for my grandson's behavior," Mr. Hiroki said.

"So, your grandson shot up my house?"

"Please understand. The violin was my grandson's to inherit. I'd almost convinced him that you weren't involved, and on the news, it said that you once went to jail for stealing a musical instrument in Miami years ago."

"If your grandson kills us, you'll hurt the people trying to help you get Buttercup back!"

"My family's attachment to the Stradivarius is more than just personal. My ability to support my family depends on how I sound when I play. That violin made me one of the most recognized violinists in the world, Henry. My family is as devastated as I am." Mr. Hiroki grabbed the handkerchief from his jacket pocket and wiped the sweat off his brow.

I faced the distraught violinist, "Henry doesn't have Buttercup. None of us do!" I stated.

"So why are you all hurrying out of town? Fleeing from the police?" Mr. Hiroki questioned. "Your husband is an ex-con! The police and the news have informed the world of that much.”

“I learned my lesson many years ago,” Henry said. “The Jazz Symphony is performing a tribute to Benny Goodman. I set up a meeting with Charlie, an expert in instruments on the black market.”

“Yes, the percussionist for the PSO before Charlie McDaniels?” Mr. Hiroki questioned.

“Yes, he’s also the Director of the Orlando Jazz Orchestra, who has a show this weekend.”

Mr. Hiroki’s face reddened, and his chin went into a deep scowl. “Do you think anyone from the Orlando Jazz Orchestra took my violin?”

“I have a few questions for Charlie concerning the local black market. Do I have to continue to worry about our safety while uncovering information to return your instrument?” Henry inquired.

Suddenly, Mr. Hiroki lifted his cane and struck it hard against the pavement. The handle folded and revealed a hidden knife. “I assure you if I wanted any of you dead, you would be. I’ve stopped my grandson. I don’t want shame brought upon my family by violent actions.”

“Are you sure there isn’t anyone else in your family willing to kill us?” I asked Mr. Hiroki.

“No, my Dear,” Mr. Hiroki interrupted. “If your husband is innocent, you and your family have nothing to fear.”

Henry stared at him for a moment. “If? It would be in your best interest if you realized we all want the same thing: your violin returned.”

"You may be able to fool everyone else. But I believe you had something to do with its disappearance. Nothing gets past you; you are a conductor with ears like a rabbit. Does your word stand for anything?" Mr. Hiroki held out his hand for the Maestro to shake.

"I understand it's like someone has taken your right arm, but you have no right to scare my wife."

The car door opened, and Katie began to stroll over. "Howdy?" She greeted Mr. Hiroki

"How nice to see you again, Katie," Mr. Hiroki said as he leaned down and kissed Katie's lips. Stunned, I took a small step back to gather her senses. "I insist that if you want to continue handling my violins you must keep better company."

Shocked, Katie touched her lips. "Hold on there, Buckaroo. You can't just be kissing any ol' person these days."

Larry kicked open the Chevette door. "That's my girl you just kissed."

"She is one of the most beautiful and talented women I know. It would be a crime not to warn you to start keeping better friends."

"Thank you, I think," Katie said. "I don't know exactly how to take that."

Mr. Hiroki started back toward his van. "It would be in your best interest since my grandson lost his inheritance."

"Understood," the Maestro never did shake his hand.

CHAPTER 36

Once we arrived in Orlando, Henry drove us to a grand hotel shaped like a castle. He made a quick text on his cell phone and then announced it to everyone in the car. "I'm meeting our percussionist here."

"Should we go in with you?" Katie asked.

"Yes," Henry glanced back. "I believe you all need to meet whom I suspect of stealing the violin."

"He's not the one with the criminal background," Katie reminded.

"Please, Katie," I begged. "Try to trust my husband."

"Maybe you should open your eyes," Larry said.

Henry opened his car door, then quickly ran around the car to open my door. I exited the Chevette as Larry and Katie did. From the lobby trotted a valet at the same time, a sizeable red-headed man headed in our direction.

"Hello, Henry," greeted timpani player Charles MacDonald.

For a moment, I admired the golden strands hidden in his red locks. His goatee was slightly blonder than the wisps of hair on his head. In his left ear, he wore a diamond studded earring. He wore all black clothing right down to his patent leather shoes.

"Charles," he greeted, shaking Henry's hand.

"Maria, Katie, welcome to Orlando. And who is this?"

Charles asked, looking directly at Larry.

"Larry Hillman," Larry nodded. "I've seen you before playing a lot in the Palm Symphony Orchestra. You're quite the drummer."

"My specialty is timpani."

Larry didn't seem to understand. He just nodded again and said, "A drum is a drum to me."

"Actually," Charles led us into the grand hotel outside Disney World. "I favor many different types of drums and percussion instruments."

"We're not here to discuss your drumming," Henry interrupted.

Charles sighed. "That's good. I was a bit worried about my position with the orchestra."

"Did you bring the same drums you played with the PSO?" Henry asked.

The group walked past a giant statue of Goofy and traveled further down the hallway to the dining room filled with chandeliers and ornate gold pillars. A hostess guided them through a maze of cloth-covered tables laden with delicately folded napkins.

"Yes, I am playing in the jazz concert tomorrow night, so my drums are upstairs in my room. Why?"

Henry smiled. "Just curious."

They sat down and I felt the need to sit beside Arnie. Underneath the table, I reached out and held his hand. Larry and Katie sat directly across from us, staring at Charles.

"Why this sudden need to know if my PSO timpani is in Orlando?" Charles asked.

Henry drank down the water that the waitress had just poured for him. While she filled the other glasses, Henry spat out. "That's where you hid the violin and managed to escape undetected. That night, you were playing conga drums. You had that set with the stretched lambskin. It would have been straightforward to adjust the side, slide it over, and stick the violin inside before anyone would notice."

Charles's eyes widened in horror. "You think I stole Mr. Hiroki's violin? I can't believe it! After all these years, you would accuse me of stealing Buttercup. I don't even play strings!"

"It's worth well over four million," Larry reminded, "more than Wallace's violin from the Titanic!"

"I wouldn't do that," Charles gasped. "I play in praise bands. How would that look to the churches I play for?"

Charles seemed very angry. His face was turning red. The hairs on his neck were standing up.

"Exactly. You couldn't let it get out that you stole such valuable equipment." I reminded.

"If you'll excuse me, I need to use the restroom," Henry said.

"Oh, me, too!" I gasped.

"Please excuse us," Henry stood. For a moment, Charles leaned back, still outraged at the accusation.

"Hurry back. We need to discuss changes to next year's

schedule. I'm unsure if you know that the board has decided to set up another meeting to discuss your free concert series."

Henry grinned. "Coming, Wife."

I rose from the table and walked beside my husband down the hallway where the sign BATHROOMS was hung. Instead of going right, Henry ensured no one was watching and grabbed my arm.

"Hurry," Henry said. "I stole Charles's card key from his jacket. We've got to hurry before he knows it's missing."

We approached the elevator. Henry pressed the tenth-floor button, and the elevator rose ten flights. Once the doors reopened, we walked several feet down the hallway until we got to rooms 10-191.

Henry stuck in his key. We slid the card and watched the light turn green. Looking over his shoulder, Henry hurried inside the room as I followed him into this very dark place.

Once I found the lights, Henry headed to the timpani drums underneath the giant two-pane window. He began to examine them. Quickly, I flicked on the lights and watched him examining the drum.

"Do you see anything?" I asked.

Suddenly, a smile creeps across Henry's face. Slowly, he turned the timpani drum around, revealing a fabric panel that appeared like wood and easily slid over.

"It looks like we found a thief," Henry whirled one of the Timpani drums around to show me the door that slid over. "He hid the violin in here while the rest of us were worried about Katie."

Suddenly, comfort washed over my body. This horrible disaster was about to come to an end. It was true Charles MacDonald had been the one that stole Mr. Hiroki's violin.

My husband was innocent.

As I hurried to the timpani to see the wood-painted fabric, I peered deeply into the drum, discovering its contents were empty. Then, suddenly and without warning, the door to the hotel room banged open.

Charles MacDonald stood in the doorway. His face is very red. "It's not what you think."

"It doesn't matter what we think," I said. "It's time to call the police."

"Don't," Charles said. Then he sat on the corner of the bed and said, "I stole the violin. You should know, Henry, since you are the one that helped me."

CHAPTER 37

"He's lying," Henry spat out.

Suddenly, Charles came forward with a fist, ready to strike Henry in the face. Henry ducked with the first swing and then punched Charles in the stomach. Falling backward, Charles reached and grabbed Henry by the jacket.

They fell onto the ground. Katie rushed forward and tried to pull Charles back, away from Henry. Charles jumped to his feet and shoved Katie onto the bed. It was then I realized that I stood between Charles and the doorway.

His eyes tightened on me.

Katie roared, "Let the Maestro go."

Larry suddenly stood in front of me, protecting me. "Don't even think about it."

"What are you going to do about it, Baldie?" Charles grumbled.

"I believe my husband is innocent," I said. "So, who helped you?" I asked Charlie.

Henry slowly got back onto his feet. He was bleeding from his lips. A part of me wanted to run over to him and ensure he was okay. Then the other side realized that Charles had just somehow admitted that Henry was involved.

"You are a fool, Maria!" Charles wiped his cheek with a cut on the side. He glanced down at Henry, who was now rising to stand. "You're his secret gem about to shine and

"

deserve more than an ex-con." Charles moved toward Maria, leaned down, and kissed her cheek.

Before his lips could move closer to Maria's lips, Larry whirled Charlie around and began to kick him in his stomach. Several times, he kicked until Charlie dropped to the ground, spitting blood.

"Where is the violin?"

"I don't know anymore," Charles suddenly revealed. "I was supposed to sell it to Anna Young when I got back to the hotel room; neither the violin nor Anna Young was here! Then I got the message that they thought Henry had stolen it."

"Is that who broke into my house and tried to kill me and my wife?" Henry asked.

"I'm guessing," Charles said. "Nice cut."

"You, too," he felt his chin.

"Okay," I gulped. "So, you drugged Katie, stole the violin, tried to sell it on the black market, but someone stole it from you instead."

Charles smiled through bloody teeth. "That seems to be the sum of things."

"If you don't have the violin, Anna Young doesn't have it, we don't have the violin, and Mr. Hiroki certainly doesn't have his instrument, then who does?" Henry suddenly asked. "And why do they want me to look like the guilty one?"

Katie jumped to her feet. "Who drugged me, Charlies?"

"I don't know," Charles admitted. "All I know is the dart

came from the winds section. Maybe from a clarinet or an oboe.”

“So, it came from the winds.” Katie rushed across the room and slapped his face. “I could have died! Who was it?”

Charles tried to rise to his feet, but this time he stumbled back. “I think I need a hospital. I’m scared, Katie. Stop being so mean.”

Katie gasped. “You are going to jail for your part in this. I could have been killed. Maria and Henry were nearly shot to death in their own home. How much was all this for?”

“The sale was for five million,” Charles said. “But I was going to donate some to the orchestra for your free concert series. I never thought I’d be found out or that you would be suspected as the thief first.”

Henry sat down on the bed. “You made peace with yourself to do this because you thought you were stealing the violin for the orchestra?”

“For all of us,” Charles said. “I could have paid off my debts, put a million in the bank, and financed your series, too. I wanted to do this for my friends. Mr. Hiroki is rich enough. That Anna Young kid is considered one of Japan’s most talented violin students. It was a win-win situation.”

“Your reasoning leaves much to be desired,” Henry said, pulling out his cell phone.

“Who are you calling,” Larry asked.

“An ambulance,” Henry finished dialing and put the phone to his ear. “In some sick way, you’re making some sense.”

Henry walked to the corner of the room to speak on the phone. Charles glanced up at me from the floor—blood streamed from his mouth. I wondered if it was internal bleeding or if he had bitten his lip.

"I've been in the Palm Symphony Orchestra for over ten years. I did what I had to do for my family and to save us. Everyone knows the orchestra is losing money, and we are barely making a profit. I didn't want the orchestra to end." Charlie admitted. "I wanted this free series as much as Henry did."

"Becoming a thief isn't how to do it," Katie announced.

"I did it for you, too! You're one of our best singers, Katie." Charlie added. "And you, Maria, you are on next year's schedule for a duet for 'Nessum Dorma.' Did you even know that?"

Honestly, I didn't. The last Henry mentioned to me was that he was sending me for lessons so that I could study. I had no idea that he had a plan for me to sing next season.

"Don't you all see? If we get Buttercup back, we can sell it to Anna Young, and everyone wins. I get my money; the orchestra has another big season, and we can all continue with no one being the wiser."

Henry hung up the phone and traveled across the room. "The ambulance is coming."

"Did you alert the police, too?" Katie asked. "He deserves to go to jail."

"Forgive me," Charles asked Katie. "I didn't know you would have such a serious reaction. I didn't even shoot it."

"Songbird," Henry called me.

"Why don't you and Katie sing Charles a song? One I loved as a kid is by the great composer Oscar Meyer, a famous composition titled, B-A-L-O-N-E-Y."

CHAPTER 38

After the EMTs discovered that Charles had just bitten his lip, the police gave him a handkerchief to wipe away the blood, handcuffed the red-headed drummer, and took him to the county jail. We marched him out with guarded smiles, hearing the birds chirp and squirrel chatter. Katie and Larry followed the police car but left when Charles began to be fingerprinted and filled out paperwork to arrest the percussionist.

Henry and I trekked back down to the car in the parking lot.

"So now what?" I asked him. "Do you believe Charles when he says he doesn't know what happened to the violin?"

Henry nodded. "Yes, you know that the orchestra is in debt. Between the copyrights and auditorium rentals, we barely covered last year's bills and still owe next month's office rent. It's no secret that we will need more money to finance the free kids' concert series." Henry sighed. "Charles is my friend; if he had sold the violin, money would no longer be a problem."

"He doesn't seem trustworthy," I muttered, getting into the passenger's side of the car.

"Oh, but he is," Henry disagreed as he got in the driver's side of the vehicle.

Suddenly, he reached down and grabbed my hand. Slowly, he lifted it to his lips and lightly kissed my fingers. He glanced at me for a moment before he lowered his grasp and turned the engine on with a key. Butterflies fluttered in my stomach. My heart skipped a beat; every moment with Henry felt wonderful, almost like I had known him for years.

"So where do we search next? If we don't find out who stole the violin from Charles, everyone will still believe that you are behind the theft. We must find Buttercup!" I added softly.

"I'm not so sure Larry or Katie believe that I wasn't somehow involved," Henry admitted. "But we are going to find it. Since Hiroki's son came after us, they don't have the violin. Charles had it stolen, leaving only one person who knows of the theft."

"The person who blew the dart!" Maria realized.

"Exactly," Henry agreed. "Charles claims he didn't know who shot the dart."

"He said it was someone in the horn section."

"I find that odd," Henry commented. "The horns face west, and yet Katie was struck when walking west. So, whoever would have shot the dart must have turned around to face east."

"We should watch the video again."

"I'm not sure our house is safe until we can return the violin to its rightful owner," Henry warned.

Maria grimaced as her eyes filled with tears. "So, we are on the run."

"For now," Henry said, pulling off onto an exit surrounded by palm trees. "We have exactly two weeks before I must be at rehearsals for Beethoven. We can't risk being attacked. They think we were involved and are in danger until we prove them wrong." After a pause, he added, "I have a funny feeling, though, that we are on the right track."

"Whoever shot the dart is the last piece to this puzzle. He knew that Charles would hide the violin in his drum and sneak it out. He double-crossed Anna Young and possibly sold it to someone else."

"I know something a bit unusual about one of the winds," Henry said.

My gaze tightened on his face. Henry had a worried expression on his face, which made his eyebrows squint as he turned the vehicle back onto the highway. Then I realized he wasn't going north on I-95, which would have returned us to our town. He was headed south. "Where are we going?"

"The airport," he replied. "We need to go a place a little farther north than Florida. The winds player lives in Canada in the summer."

"Canada!" I gasped, knowing whom he was referring to.

"Heather, the clarinetist, the one married to the hockey player. She comes here in the winter because her husband is on the road so much. She also knows an art dealer," Henry recalled.

"But art isn't the same as instrument dealings," Maria reminded.

"They go hand-in-hand," Henry said. "Most dealers handle things that would go into auction, and instruments are often included in art sales. The Stradivarius is a piece of art."

"You know that because of your dealings?" Maria asked.

"I am not a perfect man," Henry said. "I covered up things but paid my dues and would never steal an instrument for profit anymore."

"Even if it meant that your free concert series could be postponed?"

"We're flying to Canada. I have Heather's address in my phone, along with all the other instrumentalists in the winds and horn sections. We won't stop until we research every instrumentalist and see if their activities are suspicious." Henry smiled. "Unless you'd rather I leave this matter with the police."

"And let them have all the fun?" I replied to the question.

"So, you're with me?" Henry asked, smiling.

"To the end."

"Thank you for supporting me," Henry said. "You won't regret this. We will get to the bottom of this puzzle."

"I have to admit this is exciting but also scary."

"I'll protect you." Henry said, "I promise."

"You mean that, don't you?"

"I love you, Maria," Henry murmured.

"You believed in me and stuck by me even after learning about my criminal background. We are family, and I will never let harm come to you. You have my word. Whatever happens or whatever we find out, we are in this together." Henry grabbed my hand again.

I smiled back and tightened my grasp.

CHAPTER 39

On the plane, Maria's heart began to pound. She felt a little faint as she fastened her seat belt. Henry reached over and grabbed her hand. It didn't take him long to notice that she was shaking.

"Remember, you've flown before." Henry remembered.

"I know, this is such a long flight."

"Flying is safer than being in a car," Henry laughed, "especially that Chevette."

"Stop ragging on my favorite car," she leaned back. "And you are just trying to distract me from the fact that we will take off soon."

"True," he kissed her hand. "Tell me about your first car again, the one you drove for 14 years."

"Back then, they didn't have emission restrictions, so smoke came out the back exhaust from burning oil. The doors were welded shut and there were rust holes in the floor that I covered up with mats," Maria laughed. "When someone new got into the car, I had to warn them not to press down hard on the floor."

Henry leaned in. "You sure have come a long way."

"I parked once on the street and one of my college-age friends backed out from the grass and accidentally dented the side door. She was apologetic and wanted to give me money for the dent."

"What did she offer?" Henry questioned.

"Fifty dollars, and you know what I said," Maria laughed harder. "Don't bother. It's just one more dent."

The plane's engine reverberated loudly, and Maria hardly noticed she was laughing so hard. Henry grasped her hand, holding it tighter, as the passenger plane began to take off down the runway.

Suddenly, Marie's smile dropped, and she gazed fearfully into Henry's eyes. She grasped her cross necklace with her free hand and whispered, "I am with you always."

"He is, and so am I," added Henry.

The plane climbed and straightened out. Maria finally took a deep breath.

"Afraid to fly?" the woman seated to Maria's left asked, then she lifted her hand and Maria realized she was holding Henry's hand and this woman's as well.

"Oh, I'm sorry."

"Don't be. My name's Colette. I'm going to Canada to have a little gambling spree right over the border." The woman grinned widely, anticipating her holiday.

Maria studied the attractive older woman. She had blonde spiked hair with a streak of pink in it. She was dressed professionally and had a charming smile that seemed to light up the plane.

"Thank you so much for holding my hand through this scary experience. I will never forget your kindness when I am so afraid of flying."

Colette smiled. "You know we're going to go over the mountains. We'll see Niagara Falls, so this will be an amazing flight! Enjoy the view, and don't worry, God's in control."

"Yes, thank you so much for understanding."

"Who is that handsome fellow, and does he have a father who's single?"

Maria laughed, "Oh, this is Henry."

"My father has passed on," Henry explained. "But he was a boxer. A wonderful man."

"I bet he was a hunk, too," Colette said.

Henry leaned his head back and closed his eyes. Maria and Colette spoke for hours about paintings and music, strangers becoming friends amid turmoil as the plane flew over West Virginia.

"Look down there," Colette said. "There's a man on top of that mountain."

Maria quickly leaned across to squint out of the window. "Where?"

"Down there! Don't you see the man on the mountain?"

"Where? I don't see him, Colette."

"There! He's there. You can even see his beard," Colette laughed.

It was then Maria realized Colette was pulling her leg. "Is Bigfoot beside him? Please ask him if he's got a violin named Buttercup?"

"What violin?" Colette asked.

Maria told her the entire story in the fourth hour of the flight while Henry slept. Even surprising to Marie was that Colette knew the PSO clarinet player.

"How do you know her?"

"Heather is quite known in Canada in the town where I vacation. Her husband is well…he's different."

"A logger, right? Who plays hockey during the season?" Maria asked.

"A pioneer of sorts," Colette explained. "They are building an entire village in the trees. Some giant treehouses they want to become some gambling destination resort. For all those naturists, granola eater types who like to do that zip line stuff."

"Really? My husband just told me she lives in a cabin."

"It's a cabin, all right. About 200 feet high off the ground. It's called "PARADISE IN THE TREES. If you've never been there, you'll be shocked. It's about a two-story building way up in the trees."

"How do you get up there?" Maria asked.

"A giant basket lowers and lifts you. After that, zip lines are the only way to go from treehouse to treehouse. People who stay there live in the trees, like in a forest. Bears can be seen below; it's not the safest place."

Maria gulped. "I'm not sure how welcomed we will be after we question them."

"I don't think Heather was involved. She seems too nice

for that."

"You know, I never thought there could be another reason why the violin was stolen," Maria admitted. "Maybe the violin was stolen because it is made of exceptional wood!"

CHAPTER 40

The Tree Paradise was something I wasn't expecting. Standing there with my suitcase, I couldn't help but gaze upwards to take in an incredible sight. It was like a childhood fantasy of a treehouse but grander. Among giant majestic trees sat four round painted wooden treehouses connected by wooden bridges, massive as a two-storied building, each painted a muted color with dark shutters and blooming flower boxes. The slight breeze rustled the leaves and caused Maria to take a deep breath. The place was so beautiful, surrounded by giant trees. It looked like a postcard of a forest with a magical treehouse resort.

"They look like UFOs in the trees," Henry whispered.

"Let's hope we don't get abducted," I laughed.

Suddenly, Henry took a deep breath, and I noticed he wouldn't take another step forward. "Something's very wrong here."

"It's beautiful," I commented. "Don't you think? Like a giant playground for adults all in the trees."

"No," Henry gulped.

Then, suddenly, I noticed a giant wooden basket descending toward the ground. Inside was none other than the Palms Symphony Orchestra's clarinetist. I never took much notice of her, an attractive, athletic-looking tall woman with straight, multi-colored hair hanging just above her shoulders.

"Heather knew we were here," Henry announced, putting

down his carry-on case. He glanced up and pointed, "Look, cameras in all the trees. This isn't a playground; this is a fort, one that's well protected."

Heather opened the door of the giant basket she had lowered herself down in and smiled. "Why, Maestro, how nice of you to visit me with your wife, Maria!" A smile crept across her face but didn't reach her eyes.

A brilliant blue, Heather's eyes seemed unexpectedly deep set. Seriously, Maria suddenly thought to herself, could Heather be an alien? "Now I'm being ridiculous," Maria concluded. "Hi, Heather; we are sorry to arrive unannounced. We don't expect you to feed or give us a place to stay. We came to ask you a few questions about the missing Stradivarius and then we'll go to the nearest hotel."

"Buttercup?" Heather chuckled with a small snort.

"Now, why would I take Buttercup?" Heather stepped back into the basket. "Come on, I'll give you both a tour. Grab your luggage; I insist you both stay. The nearest hotel is about forty minutes away."

A chill went down my spine. Once Henry and I had gotten into the basket, Henry took my hand and whispered, "You look scared."

I faked a smile to the top.

Heather opened the basket door on the other side, and we all stepped right onto the deck of the first of the four two-story treehouses. Glancing down, I felt dizzy. We were over a hundred feet off the ground, and that plunge could kill if the giant branches didn't first break a person in two.

We traversed inside the first wooden structure. Inside were lights, a kitchen, sofas, and stairs leading up to the second-story queen-sized bed -fully equipped accommodations.

"This is where I live with my husband," Heather said. "We like living off the land and he's off hunting deer right now."

"Guns? You have guns?" I questioned.

"Yes," Heather laughed. "Why are you acting so scared of me? I assure you. I had nothing to do with the dart or the stealing of the violin. Now follow me out the back door and we'll go to the second treehouse where you both will stay. It's quite pleasant in the trees. At night, the wind howls through the leaves, as if you are a part of the tree itself."

"Great," Henry smiled. "I've always wanted to be a tree."

"The Stradivarius is made from unique maple, spruce, and willow wood. The maple tree is only found in that small part of the world, which is why that violin sounds so particularly different from all the rest."

"Yes, it is a scarce wood, and especially due to the tree's age, cut down just at the right time so that the violin will have the fullest sound." Henry nodded to explain this fact.

Henry and I followed Heather outside and stepped onto the thin wooden bridge connecting the first two treehouses. Heather didn't look down but noticed Henry grinning and gazing down.

"This is absolutely gorgeous," Henry concluded. "I've never seen anything quite like this. You really have a unique neighborhood."

"Yes," Heather said. "This is the most beautiful place on earth, right here among the trees, away from everything."

"Not music, I hope," Henry said.

"Of course, we have music. The trees love it when I play. In fact, I usually play right there on the edge, and you can see how the branches of this tree have curled down to be close to where I play.

I gasped, "Okay, this is getting really scary," Maria said, taking every step very close to the next.

"Strolling won't help you if the bridge collapses," Heather laughed.

I heard a creaking below my feet, "This is a solid bridge?" Another weird screeching noise sounded.

"It's just the wood adjusting to your weight," Heather concluded. "We're almost there."

Just then, I stepped up onto the ledge of the second treehouse. This one was even larger than the first. Its glass front doors showed etched vines crawling up the sides. The door handles were carved of spruce wood and as we approached the doors opened automatically.

"You have electricity in all four houses?" Henry asked.

"Yes, everything, even water and a working toilet," Heather said. "My husband and I spend a lot of time out here. It's very isolated and he loves the quietness."

Heather raised her arms to the ladder in the center of the room, "There is a queen bed up there for the both of you. I make breakfast at 8 if you'd like to join my husband and me."

"A real bed and breakfast in the trees," Henry commented.

"We normally charge guests," Heather explained. "But since you are my Maestro, I certainly wouldn't charge you, considering all you've done for me."

"What is the going rate?"

"It's $275 a night but includes all meals and the zip-line adventure the next morning."

"What's a zip line?" Maria asked.

"You dangle from a wire and swing among the trees like Tarzan," Henry answered for Heather.

"That's one way to put it," Heather chuckled, then turned to Maria. "Are you game? We have thrill seekers who like going down 100 feet at over 30 miles an hour."

"I'll pass," Maria said with a fearful gulp.

Henry suddenly grinned, "Oh, I'm so ready for this. Can we do it right after breakfast?"

Maria reminded, hopefully, "Aren't we just here to ask a few questions and go back to the hotel?"

CHAPTER 41

Henry's adventurous side took over any rational thinking, I believed. Heather and he got along very well, and I probably would have been jealous, but I liked Heather, too. She was very environmentally conscious and a fantastic graphic artist. As we traveled over the bridge and back into our tree abode for the evening, she explained how all the wood had been gathered from fallen trees; none came from "murdered" trees. The water was even recycled rainwater, which had been treated and the power came from solar panels on top of the roofs.

"If you live in the first house, the second is for guests, who are in the third and fourth?" I asked.

Heather stopped on the bridge and turned around. The wooden bridge swayed in the wind, making Maria very uncomfortable. "The third is also for guests; we have a newlywed couple there for this week and the last is for storage and supplies. It also has an office we use.

"This is one of the most amazing places I have ever seen," Henry announced. "I'm so glad that we decided to visit."

"We are here to question Heather," Maria reminded.

Heather turned around and started back toward the second treehouse. "There is no need for that. I don't even play violin and my husband makes plenty of money playing hockey. Why would I take it at all?"

Suddenly, Maria glanced back to Henry, who was peering over the side of the bridge, completely in awe of the view of a thin waterfall that dropped several stories onto an outcrop of rocks and then gurgled into the stream.

"Do you have trails down to the waterfall?" Henry asked.

"Yes, we have three hiking trails. One takes you right down to the rocks and we have a covered picnic table about 30 feet farther down the path with a grill."

"Wow!" Henry exclaimed. "This is paradise."

"We believe that artifact dealer Anna Young may be a buyer on the black market," Maria reported to Heather. "Charles, the timpani player, explained that Anna may have double-crossed him after he had stolen the violin and stuffed it inside a timpani drum."

Heather stepped onto the deck of the second treehouse and waited until we both had done the same. She appeared surprised at what Maria had just said. Her hands were clasped on her hips, and her eyes closed. "I can't believe it."

"Yes," Maria concluded.

"So, Anna Young had it stolen from Charles, and Henry took the blame from everyone because of his past," Heather repeated as she understood.

"You can see why we are so pressed to find the violin." Henry admitted, "The police have identified me as their main suspect, and quite frankly, I don't want to go to jail."

"Hiroki's grandson came onto our property and tried to kill us because of what the police released about Henry's past," Maria explained. "He shot at us, believing that we were guilty. If it weren't for Hiroki stopping him, we'd both be dead now."

Heather took a few steps and sat on a wooden bench against the railing of the treehouse. Slowly, she took a few deep breaths. Her face no longer looked shocked but dismayed. "Oh, this has gotten out of hand. This could destroy the reputation of the Palms Symphony Orchestra."

"If we don't find the violin, there is no telling if Hiroki will sue the orchestra for the four million dollars. The police now know Charles is the one who stole the violin, but they don't know two crucial things: 1. Who blew a dart at Katie and 2, what happened to the Stradivarius violin," Henry explained.

Heather looked Henry right in the eyes. "Did Charles say anything about who blew the dart?"

"No," Henry said. "All he knows is that it came from the wind section."

Heather's hands clasped in front of her, and sat on her lap, "So that's why you two are here."

Maria slowly lowered herself to sit beside her. "I am sorry that we must ask you questions. You are critical to the Palms Symphony Orchestra, Heather. Your position is not in jeopardy even if you were involved."

"What?" Maria gasped.

"I don't want any more musicians getting arrested. Charles was enough. He told me he wanted to sell the violin to Anna so that my free concert series could be financed," Heather gazed forward.

"Charles is very loyal to you, Henry, and to the orchestra," Heather reminded. "We are like a family. He believed in your dreams enough to steal for you to make them happen!"

"I never wanted this. If you were involved, you need to tell me. I won't inform the police about your involvement as long as we return the violin to Hiroki," Henry added.

Heather stood. "I am loyal, too," with that, she quietly walked away, leaving Henry and Maria alone, staring at each other on the treehouse deck.

CHAPTER 42

Henry didn't bother to unpack. He plopped our suitcases on top of a dresser and looked through his own. "I think I brought a flashlight, so once the lights go out in Heather's treehouse, we'll need to sneak past the third one and go all the way to the top."

"To the fourth house?" I asked. "Why there?"

"If Heather has guests in three, then the violin wouldn't be hiding there. It would be in the storage unit." Henry replied.

Maria sat on a white-painted, wooden rocking chair and swayed. "This is such a beautiful place."

"My instincts may be wrong," Henry said, "but since we know the dart came from the wind section, it must be from her."

"Or about a dozen other people," Maria smiled.

"No, if it came from the Winds, it was from Heather. The clarinet has a wide enough space for a projectile dart, and… quite frankly, there is something not right about Heather."

"She does appear slightly different," Maria admitted. "I thought maybe it was imagination but when she turns, there is some sort of reflection or…in her eyes…it's almost creepy."

Suddenly, Henry chuckled. "Maybe she is an alien, after all."

"Not an alien," Heather smiled, "but not normal either. Perhaps she had some botched plastic surgery."

Henry picked up his cell phone and dialed a number. "Yes, get me, Detective Williams, please."

There was a pause and then Henry spit out, "Did the hospital ever determine what was in that dart? Okay, well, when you find out, please let me know. Maria and I are in Canada checking on some leads with the clarinetist."

Maria couldn't hear what was being said by the detective.

"Yes, she is in the video. Can you slow-motion it and see exactly where the dart came from? If it passed her, that would mean it came from the oboe or directly from the second row, the third seat to my left." Henry hung up and turned to Maria. "He's checking. I have a powerful feeling that Heather is the one who shot the dart."

"How can you be so sure?" Maria asked. "I know she is a bit unusual, but if she cares so much for the environment, why would she hurt a human? That doesn't make sense."

Henry slowly sat down beside her in another white rocking chair. "You know, you're right."

Maria patted his hand and gazed deeply into his hazel eyes. "Instead of worrying about this, maybe we should just relax and enjoy ourselves for a few days. This is a beautiful vacation spot; you could go zip lining in the morning."

As their two lips almost met, the phone interrupted what could have been a very romantic kiss. Henry grunted and then answered, "This had better be good…oh, yes, thank you for checking. Really? That's a bit odd. Fine, yes, do you need the address? Already have it, okay? See you in the morning then."

Maria sat up. "What's going on?"

Henry turned to her, "Williams reviewed the tape. The police had to have it blown up but apparently, there is no doubt that the dart came out of the clarinet. Heather stuffed something in the front of her dress in a pocket. They are positive and have it on tape. Williams is on his way here, and…I can hardly believe what else he told me."

"What's that?" Maria questioned.

"Her I.D. is fake. There is no record of her anywhere, even her birth records. And he said the hospital had to send part of the sample away from the dart. They think it is organic, like from a frog."

"Oh my!" Maria gasped.

Henry slowly wrapped his arms around Maria and gazed down at her face. His hands moved across her cheek, turning the tightened clenched jaw into a smile. "I knew it was her, and now the detectives believe it, too. Williams is working with the Canadian police on extradition papers. He'll be here in the morning with a Mountie to arrest her.

"She's just so…nice," Maria said.

"Why would she try to hurt Katie, and why take the violin when she plays a woodwind instrument? It still doesn't make sense to me," Maria admitted. "What is her motive in all of this? Is it what the violin is worth? Four million dollars, perhaps?"

"No, I don't think so. Her husband makes enough playing hockey to build all of this."

"This is a place that would make money, not lose it,"

Maria knew. "So why did Heather attack Katie with a poison dart?"

"It wasn't meant to hurt her, only paralyze her temporarily, long enough for Charlie to carry out his plan of sticking the violin in the fake third timpani drum with Charlie none the wiser for taking the opportunity."

"So, you believe Charlie? That he didn't know about the dart?" Maria questioned quickly.

"Yes, I do," Henry smiled. "Charlie wanted the money to help me with the Free Concert series. He's had a crush on Katie for a long time. No, Charlie wouldn't want harm to come to Katie."

Suddenly, a knock came at the wooden door, but before Maria could rise to her feet, the door swung open, and there stood Katie and Larry. Maria gasped. "Katie and Larry?"

"Guess who just got married?" Katie laughed. "No better time than the present to have a honeymoon right here in 'Paradise in the Trees.'"

Maria sat back down, her mouth gaping open. Henry saw how shocked she was, and that happiness was not Maria's expression.

"Congratulations," Henry shot across the room and extended his hand to Larry. "Very happy for you both."

CHAPTER 43

Henry leaned over and patted Maria on the shoulder. "Are you all right?"

Tears flooded Maria's eyes. "I…I…I am happy for you both," but her crying didn't hide her pain, the cringing tight-lipped mouth, and closed eyes.

Larry stepped forward and knelt in front of her. "I love Katie. You are okay with us. You said you were okay with this. Not that it would have stopped me from marrying Katie, but I need to know that you are okay with all this."

"You're happy?" Maria asked after blowing her nose.

"Yes, as happy as you are," Larry replied. "I understood that you two do love each other."

"That isn't in question," Henry stated. "Songbird and I are very much in love and very happy. Even then, I knew how long you and Katie dated and that it must be tough."

Suddenly, Maria wiped her eyes, reached up, and hugged Larry. "Of course, it is unexpected for me, but I am very happy for you both."

"Congratulations, Katie," Henry reached over to hug Katie, and she smiled. "All right, then, that's all settled. We're married. You two are married. Everyone's happy, so let's get down to business. We chose to honeymoon here to find the violin and arrest the person who shot that dart!"

"We are pretty sure that Heather was involved," Maria said with a little sniffle.

"Yes, I gathered as much since you made plane reservations to Canada. It makes sense too that the dart would come out of the woodwinds section. Heather has never been a fan of mine."

"I didn't even know you two knew each other," Maria sighed.

"Oh, yes, we go a long way back all the way to Community Chorus when I met her then-boyfriend. He asked me out right in front of her, and it didn't go over well. She threatened me in the parking lot, and I gave her a shove. It took several years before Heather got over it although now, I wonder if she ever has," she tagged softly.

"You're kidding?" Henry questioned. "Why haven't I ever heard of this?"

"It was a long time ago but Heather sure was happy when I called to announce I had just gotten married to Larry. She gave us the treehouse for nearly half off and free breakfast in the morning."

"I am finding this very hard to believe," Maria said, "that she would let all of us stay here so cheaply."

"Do you think she is trying to fool us into believing she wasn't behind the dart attack?" Larry asked.

"Look!" Katie interrupted.

The group turned around and walked to the glass window near Katie overlooking the first treehouse. Heather sat in the basket, lowering herself to the ground. A few seconds later, a car engine purred to life.

"She's leaving," Katie surmised.

"Excellent!" Henry smiled.

"Yes, now we can explore the storage room at the top," Maria explained.

"We're going up there," Katie pointed to the highest treehouse. Only silence followed for a few seconds.

"Got any better ideas?" Maria asked. "I think my husband has a great idea. If she has the violin, it would be there. Let's go find it once and for all."

"No, if she has the violin, it would be in her own house," Henry interrupted. "Let's go there first."

"We're breaking into Heather's treehouse?" Maria questioned.

Henry nodded yes, grabbed Maria's hand, and led her onto the treehouse deck, heading straight for a break-in.

The group slowly traversed the thin bridge and arrived at the back door. Henry grabbed the door handle. "It's locked," he announced, then pulled a small pocketknife from his jacket. "This should do it and she'll never know that we decided to have a peek."

The door popped open in a few seconds, and the group traipsed in. The first treehouse was far more significant than the second. It had all the comforts of home, including a big pot of tea that was steeping on the counter. Maria began to search behind cabinet doors to see if she could find the violin.

A popping noise stopped her; it seemed to be coming from a cabinet behind an intricately carved wooden door. Slowly, Maria leaned down and grabbed the unusual door. "I think I've found something," she murmured.

Katie, Larry, and Henry gathered around, watching Maria open the wooden door, which revealed a terrarium. Inside were several different colored frogs; one was bright blue and black.

"Those are toxic frogs," Henry announced. "I think we found where the poison came from."

"So it was Heather!" Katie sneered. "I should have given her a much bigger shove."

CHAPTER 44

"The frogs are so colorful," Maria noted. "I've never seen such a brilliant shade of blue and those black spots are adorable."

"Don't stick your hand in," Henry warned.

Katie leaned down and stared at them. "So, I could have been killed by these frogs?"

"Aren't they beautiful?" Maria asked. "I mean…if they weren't so deadly."

"They are," Katie huffed. "That green and red one has the cutest eyes, right?"

"That one looks a little like Kermit," Maria laughed. "Except for the giant fingertips."

"God makes creatures of all kinds," Henry leaned down. "Kind of like the way he made women."

Both Katie and Maria slowly turned their heads to stare at Henry. He grinned widely.

"What exactly are you implying?" Katie asked.

"Women can be just as beautiful and deadly," Henry chuckled.

"Here we are in this romantic place and he's joking around," Larry huffed. "I wouldn't piss off my woman now with all these frogs around."

"Funny," Katie said. Then she gazed back at the frogs. "I

should hate them all, but I just can't seem to."

"They aren't to blame," Maria reminded.

"No, they're not. Heather is the one who put the poison in the syringe enough to cause temporary paralysis for me."

"You're lucky to be alive," Henry said. "These frogs have killed grown men twice your size."

Maria stood up and began to search other cabinets. Everything was in perfect order, and books were stacked in piles in nearly every corner of the room. "She sure likes James Patterson."

"Who doesn't?" Katie smiled.

Crossing into the bedroom, Maria entered the closet. There were many clothes, primarily black, on the near side and lots of hockey equipment and uniforms for the Kodiak Flyers on the far side.

It was then that something caught Maria's interest. It was a photo album that had Henry's picture on the front. Maria opened it and to her surprise, a collection of programs from the PSO, tons of pictures of Heather playing clarinet, and after-party photos appeared. "Henry!" Maria called. "Come take a look."

The Maestro rushed into the closet and scanned the photo album. "You wouldn't think someone who loved the orchestra so much would have wanted to take Hiroki's violin."

Maria turned to the last page, and on it was a picture of Hiroki and Heather with the Stradivarius being held by Hiroki. Heather had her hand around its neck as if trying to take it. "Isn't that odd?"

"It's like Heather knew she was planning on taking it," Henry concluded.

"Why would she want the violin?" Maria gasped. "There must be some kind of clue to why and where she might have taken it."

"We've searched the whole treehouse," Katie announced. "The violin isn't here."

"Did you find any clues in your honeymoon suite?" Henry asked Katie.

"Nothing," Larry answered Katie. "We turned the place upside down and if it isn't here, then that leaves only the storage and office treehouse number four to search."

"All right," Henry agreed. "Let's hurry. There is no telling when Heather will return."

"We only have until morning," Maria reminded, "until Detective Williams arrives to arrest Heather."

"Why do I feel like something is just not right here?" Henry asked. "I still don't understand why Heather would want the violin when she doesn't play strings and, quite frankly, loves the PSO. No one would have this photo album if they hated us."

"Perhaps she's like Charlie and wanted to pay for all the free concerts out of the sale money," Maria wondered.

"Let's move before dark," Larry waved for them to come.

The group slowly traversed the three bridges and past the three buildings high in the trees to reach the last treehouse. The deck of this one was covered in moss and appeared not as well kept. Henry nearly slipped on the deck, but he kept himself from falling by grabbing onto the base of a tree limb.

Maria didn't dare look over the side. "How high do you suppose we are right now?"

"About equal to a seven-story high-rise," Larry guessed, then he took the doorknob in his hand and began picking the lock with a long pin. There was a click and Larry murmured, "Works every time."

"I can't believe you got us in this quick," Maria praised.

Then, the group entered the very dark storage treehouse. Inside were boxes and boxes stacked up to the ceiling. Two desks appeared cluttered but held no computer. Several filing cabinets lined the back of the room but showed no labels.

"This is a big mess," Henry gasped. "Remind me never to make Heather the PSO librarian."

"Not funny," Katie said. "You'd have to let her go once she's in prison."

"We aren't sure of anything other than that Heather had access to frogs, which might be pets," Henry reminded. "We haven't found the evidence to prove our case. The cops can test the frogs and see if the toxins match."

"Buttercup," Larry said.

"One of the world's most precious instruments."

"Probably one of the most famous violins in our history," Maria said. "Perhaps Heather is an alien and stole the violin to take back to her planet so that aliens can learn how to play."

Larry gave her a look like, "Really?"

Katie shook her head no. "Stay on this planet, please. We have enough toxic things to worry about right here."

"True," Maria smiled. "I'm just very thankful that whatever Heather's motives are, no one was permanently injured."

"At least not yet," uttered a deep voice.

Slowly, Henry, Larry, Katie, and Maria turned to face the source of the sound.

CHAPTER 45

Maria couldn't believe her eyes. Hiroki stood with his arms outstretched to Katie and murmured, "How could I have been so wrong? Heather made the dart, and she was behind stealing my violin. You are trying to return my instrument."

"We all are," Larry tagged. "We are just about to search the storage unit, the fourth treehouse just up the mountain."

"Detective Williams called me," Hiroki said.

"How did you get here so quickly?" Maria asked.

"I can't sleep. I can't eat. All I can think about is precious Buttercup and how even a scratch could change the quality of her sound. I must find her!" Hiroki's voice cracked with emotion.

"Did you follow us?" Katie asked, hugging him.

"Please forgive me but I can't let this go. We should all work together to get my violin back. We're getting closer. The original deal with Charlie fell through because Heather must have been working with Anna Young to steal the violin."

"And we also have figured out that the poison came from dart frogs, which Heather keeps as pets," Maria concluded.

"So, we know who was involved," Hiroki said, pleased. "Detective Williams called to tell me where he was going and would arrest Heather in the morning. All of this is excellent work, but we still lack the most important thing."

"I can guess what that is," Henry said.

"Where is Buttercup?" Hiroki whined.

"She could be anywhere," Katie said.

"By now, she could be halfway around the globe and in some horrible violinist's hands who won't know how to treat her." He moved forward, took several steps, and suddenly squinted, looking off to the side.

"Buttercup is very important to you and the entire PSO. Your being our concertmaster is a huge ticket draw and we all care for you and your family."

Hiroki took several more steps. His eyes were fixed to the left, behind the group's standing. After taking another breath, he took one more move forward. "I can't believe it."

"What is it? You look like you've seen a ghost," Katie warned. "Are you all right?"

"She's here," Hiroki gasped and rushed past the group to an oversized gray recliner chair in front of a kitchenette. He lowered his hand and held up a violin bow. One tiny horsehair dangling down. "This is Buttercup's bow. I'd know it anywhere."

Suddenly, the group started searching; Katie began looking around the kitchen. Henry knelt on the floor, looking under the recliner. Larry shuffled papers around the dirty desk and Maria lifted the chair cushion.

"It's not here," Hiroki gasped. "How could she do this? How could Heather separate the bow from Buttercup?"

"Well, she can't be far," Katie reasoned.

"Heather did steal Buttercup from Charlie for Anna

Young. Henry added that this is proof that we can show Detective Williams tomorrow," Henry added. "There is no doubt now who was behind all of this."

"Unless one of you put it there," Hiroki added, turning slowly to face the group.

"Don't be ridiculous," Maria said.

"Where would we have been able to hide a bow all this time," Katie added. "We didn't bring it here."

"When one of us turned or something," Hiroki said. "You two were here before Maria and Henry."

"All right," Henry sat in the recliner and stretched his arms. "We don't need to turn on one another at this point. So far, we found dart frogs and Buttercup's bow. At least we know that much. Pointing out doubts is just not going to get us anywhere."

"True," Maria said. "We have to go on faith that we are the ones who are trying to bring Buttercup back to its rightful owner."

"But I am just pointing out that all the suspects are here. So, the fact the bow was found proves that one of us and Heather knows where Buttercup is." Hiroki said. "At least I have the bow back."

"I don't think Buttercup is here," Larry said. "We've searched this entire treehouse and it's not."

"It could still be in the storage unit," Henry reminded.

"Then we should search there before Heather gets back. We need to have all our ducks in a row before the police return," Maria suggested.

"Quack. Quack." Henry mumbled.

Larry smiled, "Couldn't have said it better myself."

CHAPTER 46

When the group finally arrived at the dingy storage unit after a nerve-racking trek, Maria peered in the small glass windows. There was a desk, and several filing cabinets appeared against the walls. The office was surprisingly clean and organized. On the wall was a painting of a white owl with giant yellow eyes.

"Do you see anyone inside?" Henry questioned.

"No," Maria replied.

Larry quickly popped the front lock and opened the door. When the group was inside, Maria went straight to the giant white snowy owl painting. Its claws were coming straight for the viewer as if in mid-flight.

"Do you like that?" Larry asked.

"It seems oversized for the room," Maria said, "although a very stunning piece of art."

"Makes me glad I'm not a mouse," Larry muttered.

"The eyes practically glow," Henry said. "I agree. This is a very unusual piece of art."

Maria turned her attention to the personal photos next to the painting of the owl. They were of Heather and a man at their wedding. Another photo was taken at the foot of a sequoia tree, plus over pictures of natural wonders of the world such as Yellowstone National Park and the Grand Canyon.

Shifting, Maria placed her hands on the outside of the owl painting. "Can someone help me get this down from the wall?"

Henry and Larry grabbed both sides and slowly lowered the painting to the floor. Behind it appeared a safe with a wide keyhole. Maria immediately shined her flashlight inside the hole, trying to see.

"Do you see Buttercup?" Henry asked.

"I am not sure," Maria admitted, squinting. She gazed profoundly and then gasped as she saw what looked like a shiny head. "There is an instrument!"

"Step back," Hiroki grabbed the desk chair and began smashing the chair against the safe's door. "We must get in there!"

After several attempts, the safe buckled. Henry grabbed the safe door and, with all his might, pulled until the lock broke. In front of them sat a clarinet.

"We haven't found her," Hiroki grasped the clarinet, cradling it like a child. "Oh, how I miss my instrument."

Tears welled in Maria's eyes.

"She's not here," Hiroki started to cry softly.

Henry placed his hand on Hiroki's shoulder. "I hope that proves that we did everything possible to return her to you."

"Thank you," Hiroki murmured, glancing up.

"Now, we should call the police," Larry said.

"No reason to wait until morning now," Maria agreed.

"We know now that Heather stole it!"

"We certainly can't wait," Larry said. "What if Heather comes back and sees the broken safe? We will be endangered then. We need to make sure that the police know, and that Heather should be arrested."

"I'm not going to jail," said a voice behind them.

Maria knew it was Heather and gasped, "Heather!"

Hiroki whirled around and, from his cane, pulled out a narrow sword. "You will pay for this," he threatened.

"Give the clarinet back to me," Heather shouted.

"Why should you get yours back?" Maria gasped.

"Oh, like you don't know." Heather snarled.

"I don't," Maria admitted.

"She doesn't," Henry said.

"She doesn't know?" Heather asked him.

"No, she has no idea, and this has to end now," Henry said. "Heather, it's over. You can't get away now. All these people know, and you are going to go to jail if you don't let us leave. Hiroki won't press charges if you just let us go and return his violin."

Hiroki glanced up at Henry in apparent shock. "You did work with her on this, didn't you?"

"No," Henry said. "But now that there is proof that it was Heather, I know why."

Maria walked over to Henry and placed her hand around

his forearm. "What is going on? What aren't you telling us? Why did Heather steal Buttercup and lure us out here?"

"I owe Heather money for the last two seasons. I haven't been able to pay her. So, she is probably doing this for revenge."

"Oh, that's a good guess," Heather stated. "It wasn't easy watching newbies get paid while I worked. However, that proved how much the orchestra was in trouble without even the free concert series. I wanted to make sure the orchestra continued."

"By becoming a crook?" Katie asked.

"Protecting the finest instrument wood in the history of mankind," Heather said. "I found a buyer who would pay more than Anna Young. The millions would have been split between the orchestra and me."

"You were planning to screw Charlie and Anna the whole time," Katie smirked.

"And you would have forgiven me with a few more solos with the PSO," Heather snipped. "We're all for saving the orchestra and on the same side."

Silence fell as the group stared at one another realizing Heather was right.

CHAPTER 47

"The dart was supposed to have a dose of a mild sedative, not so dangerous!" Heather gasped. "Please believe me! I am so sorry, Katie," Heather said. "I didn't mean for all this to happen. I was so wrong, and it will never happen again."

"You're right," Hiroki grimaced. "Because you're going to jail."

"Hiroki, I am angry at Heather, too. If we find Buttercup, will you not press charges?" Henry asked. "It is the right thing to do."

"For you, Maestro, anything." Hiroki sheathed his sword and bowed.

Henry returned the bow, "You'll be my Concertmaster for life."

Hiroki gasped, "With pleasure."

"Katie, I ask this as your friend. Please don't press charges now that you know who shot you with a dart."

"Well, if we're bargaining, how about at least one solo every season," Katie said.

"You're vicious," Larry laughed. "Glad you're my wife and not my enemy."

Laughing, Henry smiled. "It would be my honor to have you."

"Thank you," Heather started crying. "You mean I may not go to jail after all?"

"We'll get you the best lawyer in town, Donnie Wilson," Maria said.

"Your brother?" Heather asked.

I nodded as police sirens could be heard.

"I called the police," Hiroki said. "Before the truce."

"We'll tell them just enough that no one goes to jail," Henry said. "Agreed?"

In unison, we all said, "Agreed."

"Good," Heather stated. "Now that I am no longer going to jail. I can tell you who the real buyer is."

CHAPTER 48

Heather showed me a few tricks on PowerPoint she had learned. She may look odd, but Heather's art trumps mine. We created some ads and sent them up in Dropbox for later use.

Larry and Katie left us early to go to the wedding suite. My heart physically hurt when I thought of them married. I was no longer in love with Larry but still found jealousy an issue. No matter how many years had passed, I remembered how much fun we had once.

Hiroki slept in our bed like a baby, snoring away.

It was 9 before Arnie arrived. He gave me a quick wink with his blue eyes and said, "This will be over soon. We've already got the cabin surroundings. The buyer is Jason Middles. He arrives at 10 for the violin. The money will be then wired, which we have already decided to block but document it for court."

"How did you get all this information?" I asked.

"His phone has a tap. He has no idea Heather told us everything. She discovered that Jason Middles stole the instruments in Miami, which Henry was blamed and went to jail for all those years ago."

"What can we do?" Katie, Larry, Hiroki, and I gathered in the center of the treehouse.

"You all can stay in the cruiser, which is bulletproof, while we send in the calvary. Watch from a distance."

"Can I get back my violin," Hiroki asked.

"It must be taken in to be dusted for prints and further documentation, but eventually, the violin will be returned," Arnie said.

"Then let's go," Hiroki said.

All of us went down in the basket to the armored car. I sat next to Henry, who suddenly reached out to take my hand. "You ready?"

By the time we got there, police officers and Mounties had surrounded the building. Gunfire began. When a Mountie got shot right next to the car. Larry yanked out two guns from underneath his jacket.

Hiroki unsheathed his sword. "Let's go help them out."

"No," I grabbed Henry's arm but he already had taken the gun from Larry's hand and was leaving the vehicle.

Arnie was looking in a window as the three men approached. Only two inside!" he shouted over the gunfire.

Hiroki ran at the window and burst in with his sword. Arnie and Larry began shooting and leaping in after. My heart raced, and then all I heard was silence. A few seconds had passed and out came Mounties, Hiroki, Larry, and then Henry, who looked unharmed.

"Larry looks so hot right now," Katie said.

Heather opened the vehicle door. "Did you find Buttercup?'

"No," Hiroki said.

"Come on," She nodded to me. "He has it in the basement."

We entered the cabin and walked past Jack Rhimes and another man dead on the floor from gunshots. There were puddles of blood surrounding their heads and bellies. The smell of the blood nearly made me vomit, but I chose not to look further as we traveled downstairs into the darkened basement full of boxes and spiderwebs.

Sure, enough on a table lay Buttercup.

"Don't touch it," Arnie Williams said. "Not yet."

"Oh, my baby! I've missed you," Hiroki said to the violin.

I had never been so happy to see a violin in my life.

"It's over," Henry said. "Our problems are finally gone. Jack is dead, and the violin is safe."

Heather turned to look at Henry and, with a twinkle in her eye, said, "Except for the ghost in the music library. My friends can help you with that."

Henry shook his head, "Back to that, are we?"

Heather smiled, "Yes, we got another kind of evil to eliminate."

CHAPTER 51

Several weeks had passed before we met at the office. Bradly, Heather, Henry, Jennifer, Priest Jacobs and me. We hadn't seen Larry or Katie since they decided to go to Hawaii for another honeymoon.

"Gary will be here soon," Heather said. "He has seventh sight like a medium."

"What can we expect?" Henry asked Priest Jacobs, who wore his clerical robe with a white collar.

He lowered his glasses, "I've been through many blessings, and all are different. It truly depends on if these are ghosts or demons. I need someone to light the sage as I pray and sprinkle holy water all throughout the library."

Heather took the sage out of the Priest's hand.

"The goal here is to release them to the other side," the Priest said.

"My Uncle will be going to hell," Jennifer said.

The Priest put a hand on her shoulder. "My Dear, that is not your choice. Always seek forgiveness if you want the good Lord to forgive you. I see now you may be the problem.

Your rage may be the very reason the ghost of your uncle can't move on."

"He stalks me from the grave," Jennifer's eyes teared up.

"Forgive him, please. Let the Lord decide who passes through the gates."

"I just got a text from Gary. He's stuck in traffic and maybe another hour," Heather said.

"Then we'll do the cleansing without him," the Priest announced.

"Without our leader," Bradly said. Then he put headphones on his long-haired head and held out the recorder.

"Open the door," the Priest told Jennifer.

Henry took my hand, "Are you sure you want to see this? We don't have to be here. Your brother wants to meet me for lunch to sponsor a Pulse tribute concert."

"I want to be here," I admitted.

The door opened and we all single file went into the library. Henry used a lighter and the sage smoke went up into the air.

"In the name of the Lord. We ask you to leave this place, Uncle Max," the Priest said.

Suddenly the last filing cabinet swung open and sheet music rose up and landed on top. Henry rushed over to see what it was. He studied it for a moment and said, "This isn't one of ours. It is handwritten."

"There are three of us," Bradly said. "It said three of us."

"Who are you?" Bradly yelled.

"This is written for piano and soprano voice," Henry said. "The words are quite beautiful. I shall love you throughout all time. Despite that, I had to go; my heart waits and rejoices that you love again."

"What did you just say?" I gasped, recognizing some of the words. "Did you just say I shall love you throughout all time? That is what my late husband always said to me every day."

"I am Wilson," Bradly said. "He claims his name is Wilson."

"That's our last name," I said.

"This is quite a beautiful piece of music," Henry said. "Did you write it for Maria to sing?"

"Yes," Bradly shouted. "That was a very loud yes."

"All right," Henry said. "We'll put it in next season with Maria singing it for you. I thought your husband played the violin?"

"He also played piano and harp. He loved to write music. He even sold a few piano pieces." I admitted.

"We release you to heaven. You have delivered your music. Now go in peace." The Priest concluded.

"Go play your music with the angels, Love. Thank you for the music," I said, grasping the music.

"I shall love you throughout all time…remember, and I shall go. Be happy, my love," Bradley said. "He is now saying goodbye."

Suddenly, there was a flash of light, and it was gone. "Who are the other two ghosts?" Heather asked.

Jennifer shouted, watching two orb lights flicker and then expand to human-sized figures, "Uncle Max, I forgive you. I forgive it all. Go in peace."

Suddenly standing before us was an older gentleman wearing glasses and a three-piece suit. He was clear as day. Short grey hair sat on top of his crew-cut head.

"Uncle," Jennifer recognized him. "I forgive you."

"Thank you," he said. "I am truly sorry for everything -all the pain and lies."

"I accept your apology," Jennifer reached out to take his hand, but hers went through what looked like a mist. "Are you happy where you are now?"

Beside him strutted another figure that I recognized. It was none other than Amadeus Mozart with his white hair, round eyes, and brilliant smile. Mozart put his arm about him, giggling. "Of course, Max is. He's an intern."

"Goodbye, Niece," and just as quickly as they came, they vanished—with a soft giggle from Mozart.

"I hear nothing now," Bradly announced.

The Priest nodded, "They have all gone. Our work here is done."

Heather said, "That was beautiful. Gary is sure going to be sorry he missed this."

The room seemed lighter and airy, like never before. I hugged Bradly and Heather, then the Priest. "Thank you."

"Yes, thank you, Father," Jennifer said. "I think I truly have forgiven my uncle."

Henry took a chair near the cabinet, "Is it weird that I liked having Mozart in the library? I can hardly believe I met him."

Heather put the sage in a bowl and touched his shoulder. "Mozart may return, and we'll be a haunted symphony again."

"Yes," Henry said. "I can only hope."

To donate to the Space Coast Symphony

go to www.spacecoastsymphony.org

or write

219 N Indian River Dr, Cocoa, FL 32922 ·